The Enkert Dossiers

A Novel

The Enkert Dossiers

A Novel

Edward Renehan

2015

New Street Communications, LLC

Wickford, RI

Published 2015 by
New Street Communications, LLC
Wickford, Rhode Island

newstreetcommunications.com

To the memory of
Ilse Marcus,
Survivor of Auschwitz-Birkenau

Note from the Author

During September of 1971 a small, renegade group of high-ranking ODESSA members attempted to mount a major terrorist attack within the city of Bonn, then the capital of the Federal Republic of Germany (aka, West Germany). With this action, their intent was to inspire and launch a well-funded, carefully-structured, and heavilly-armed resistance movement in opposition to the authorities then governing what they viewed as the "occupied" Fatherland of the fallen Reich. In this manner they planned to move the ODESSA from the shadows, transforming it from a relatively passive cabal of concealment and retreat which only killed when threatened, to a much-feared underground army brazenly aimed at ushering in a new era of militant National Socialism. Although well-documented in classified files held by the German government and INTERPOL, the fact that this plan ever existed remains obscure and not a matter of public record. To reveal the extent to which truth and fiction merge in the following narrative would be to destroy much of the tension and suspense which make the story intriguing. But be advised this "fiction" finds its basis in a truth all too real. - EJR

Primo Levi - *Monsters exist, but they are too few in number to be truly dangerous. More dangerous are the common men, the functionaries ready to believe and to act without asking questions.*

Genesis, 4:10 - *And the Lord said, "What have you done? The voice of your brother's blood is crying to me from the ground."*

Chapter 1

September 1971

He floored his little Aston Martin DB5 – his pride, his favorite toy. The machine cut quickly through the green countryside. He'd opened both the driver and passenger side windows. The breeze tossed Jurgen's hair this way and that. He was glad for the shrill coolness. The previous hours in Munich had been blisteringly hot – in fact the hottest morning of the hottest September on record in that city.

He'd been miserable sitting in his father's decrepit little flat with just one slow fan turning. The old man – if one could apply that description to a man aged just sixty (and in the case of Jurgen's father, one certainly could) – the old man smelled of many days' sweat. His fingernails were dirty, his hair long and greasy, and his beard ragged. Hygiene, it seemed, was no longer much of a priority with him. He dwelt mentally and physically far, far away in time, space, and experience from the sharply-dressed SS trooper whose photograph Jurgen's mother had cherished, and of whom she'd taught her son to be so proud. The man's more than twenty-five years away had broken him. His furtive eyes resembled those of an animal. A wary and hunted animal.

The visit was painful, though in the end Jurgen got what he needed.

"You are here," his father had said, opening the door a crack. "I recognize you. All this long time and I still recognize you."

"Yes."

"How did you find me?"

"Never mind. I found you."

"How did you learn I was back?"

"Never mind. I learned."

The man grunted in understanding, then he opened the door wider. He spoke plainly, and without excitement.

"It is good to see you," he said, as if admitting something quite unexceptional. "I thought I would not see you. I did not know where to look."

They did not embrace. They did not even shake hands, although there was no bad intent in this. It just did not seem natural for either of them.

The old man gestured toward a half-broken couch.

"Sit."

Jurgen's father appeared neither happy nor sad to see him. It was as if Jurgen's presence represented just one more new, puzzling, and potentially disturbing fact to be accepted and digested, one among thousands in a world the old man no longer recognized.

The father sat down on a stiff wooden chair across from the couch.

"I was sorry when your mother died, although I did not find out till a long time later. I was in Chile then. After that I did not know what became of you."

"I was eight. Tante Lisel Schmidt took me to Bonn."

The old man digested this.

"Agh. Lisel. The bereaved war widow with all her complaints. All her hatred of her own people. Her own family. And now you are grown."

"Yes. Now I am grown."

The old man nodded.

"I know it is very dangerous for me to be back here. But I don't care. If I am found, I am found. I am told I do not have long, and I want to die in Germany, not out there." He waved his hand half-heartedly, as if indicating the street, even though he wasn't.

Jurgen looked about the squalid one-room apartment. Paint peeled from the walls. Water stains scarred the ceiling. Flies buzzed in the kitchenette. And a dank, pungent aroma arose out of the bathroom. Jurgen guessed the broken couch on which he sat did double-duty as his father's bed. A small television rested on the table. Beside that a battered radio.

"And this?"

The old man shrugged.

"I know. Not grand. But believe me – this is a palace compared to what I'm used to."

"How did you find it?"

The old man shrugged again.

"Some friends get the place for me, and help me with a little money. I think a Jew owns the building. Anyway, he looks like a Jew. I only saw him when he gave me the key. My friends pay him the rent, and they send me a little money for food. I have enough. After all, I am not a terribly important person. I have to be content with crumbs. I am used to that. I have always been used to that."

"You deserve better," Jurgen lied.

"Well," his father said, "such is the world. But never mind. Let's talk of something else. Does Lisel know you have come here?"

"I am not in touch with her," Jurgen answered, lying once again. "I grew up and got out. I got sick of her telling me all the time what villians my family were."

"She was always soft – *if a bitch can be soft*. She never undertood realities. She and Germans like her are the reason the Reich failed. I'm glad you figured this out."

Jurgen marveled at how easily the old man slid into the belief that father and son stood united on the same side of history. Could it really be this simple? Yes, considering his father was not very bright and also had little idea of the mindset of postwar Germany, having never lived in it until the last week or so.

"Anyway," the old man continued. "So why have you come? What can I do for you?"

"You are here. Maybe not for long. I want to know you," Jurgen said. "I want to talk. I want to understand. I want to learn about my family. My *real* family, and all that went on."

"There is a great deal to understand. There are so many lies. Alright. A seminar then. I will speak freely. There is nothing they can do to me anymore."

And so it proceeded. For more than three hours. Hours full of revelations Jurgen found repulsive, and opinions with which he did not argue. Still, that was all for the good. In the end, Jurgen got what he'd come for.

Now he was glad and grateful to be gone from there. Grateful too for the fresh air – for the farms and pastures and mountains.

Driving the autobahn between Munich and Berlin was like taking a tour through the history of the fallen Reich – first Nuremberg, then Dresden in East Germany, and finally the old capital itself. Now, more than twenty-five years after what had at first been thought of as defeat (a defeat he was too young to truly remember), all of these were completely new, rebuilt cities.

Here were modern skylines erected upon rubble, even though sometimes still surrounded by medieval walls. To the distant east, somewhere over there, fragments of Hitler lay in a plastic body-bag: a desiccated carcass reduced to charred black meat and bone. Cinders. At Berlin, the Führer's largely forgotten, broken bunker cowered in the shadow of the Wall – partly destroyed, partly flooded, but still (the bravely curious said) a chamber of haunting echoes, echoes which seemed far more ancient and savage than nostalgic.

Jurgen much preferred his native Bonn to Berlin. He considered the new capital a symbol of the better Germany: a city epitomizing promise; a city happily bereft of ghosts. At least the worst ghosts. In fact, he did not see the point of Berlin at all. He thought, secretly, the little island on the west side of the Wall should probably just be surrendered to the dismal Red sea by which it sat surrounded.

Symbols were stupid. And expensive. Besides, the symbol of West Berlin seemed a bit too precarious and tentative. A worm-eaten apple dangling from the bough, and an autumn wind blowing. Would it really be worth going to war over? *Ich bin ein Berliner?* Well *no*, actually. JFK had *not* been a Berliner. And now he was a citizen of nowhere, laying nearly eight years already under a flame that was no more eternal than anything else of this world.

Throughout the second half of his journey, as he gained on Berlin, the country became dismal: that grim no-man's land in between Dresden and the old capital. Watch-towers overshadowed the highway throughout Thuringia, Sachsen-Anhalt, and Branden-burg. Men with machine guns surveyed the terrain. Tall, barbed wire fencing abutted the road. Massive stumps dotted the landscape. One could visualize the vast aged forest which had once been – all of it now decapitated for a mile or more on either side of the autobahn, although still present in the far distance.

This was what Hitler had brought to Germany. Or, at least, what he had invited the Soviets to bring. *So much for your messiah, my father.* The whole of the drive took him six hours.

*

The King Frederick Hotel. One of the few surviving prewar structures on the Kurfürstendamm. A rare neo-Gothic brick castle of yearning spires, wide decorative arches, leering gargoyles, and large atriums.

In Hitler's day, the 1880s building had been scheduled for demolition. It did not fit into architect Albert Speer's great master plan for the future Berlin – the Berlin which he and his Führer envisioned as *Germania*, the grand Teutonic epicenter of the Thousand Year Reich.

Today the bold Victorian seemed quite out of place: a proud, antique curiosity amid the glass, steel and concrete of the modern era – the buildings which had grown up atop the leveled Berlin of 1945. At least above the leveled *West* Berlin.

As for Speer's stark vision, several iconic examples still stood not far away: the main terminal of the
Tempelhof Airport, the Waldbühne open-air arena,
the Zoologischer Garten rail station, and of course the
majestic Olympic Stadium where in 1936 the American sprinter Jesse Owens had done more than anyone to contradict Hitler's twisted notion of a "master-
race." Here and there on each of these buildings you
could detect slight shades and shadows revealing
where prominent swastikas had once been displayed.
But the King Frederick showed no such blemishes.

The flag of the Republic blew in the breeze above
the hotel's main entrance. Jurgen came to a stop beneath it. He chuckled as a teenaged parking attendant
eagerly took the keys to the Aston and roared off
toward the establishment's parking garage. The boy
grinned widely, obviously delighted to be at the
wheel of such a fine machine. Carrying his overnight
bag, Jurgen entered the plush lobby and made
directly for the bar to the rear of the building, *Die
Macht des Schwertes*.

The bar was sparsely lit and well attended. Ro-
tund men in grey business suits drank and smoked
and spoke in low tones, making deals and planning
strategies. Newly arrived tourists cheerfully ordered

German microbrews and swilled them down faster than anyone should. Several soldiers – American – took up a corner booth where they shared bloody marys with a few extremely well-put-together, de-lightedly-laughing young ladies.

Kreigsman sat where he said he'd be, at the far end of the bar, quite alone and quite in the shadows. Kreigsman looked up as Jurgen approached. He smil-ed and motioned for the younger man to sit down on the stool beside him.

"You are thirsty," he announced, with no prelim-inary. Waving to the nearest bartender, he shouted: "Schnapps for my friend. And another for me."

Kreigsman wore his gray hair brushed back. With this, and his immaculately-groomed white beard, he looked for all the world like Hemingway. His tan was healthy, his body trim, his handshake hearty and firm, and his smile genuine. He wore a sharply tail-ored black suit. It was so hard to believe he was the same age as Jurgen's father. He resembled at a glance the man he actually was: a cultured, robust, wealthy retiree who had once sailed single-handed around the entire island of Britain, and who now owned his own small river sloop on which he explored the Danube with great regularity.

"You made good time?" he asked. "You had a pleasant journey?"

Jurgen nodded.

The drinks came and Kreigsman made a toast.

"To success," he said.

"To success," Jurgen repeated.

"And here we are in Berlin," Kreigsman sighed. "I hate Berlin. The Wall. The mood. Everything. No, Vienna is my town now. I dislike ever to leave it. A beautiful city, wonderful music, great history. As for you, I'm sure you'd rather be back in Bonn."

Jurgen thought of Ruth, and smiled.

"So, let's double-check. Who are you?" Kreigsman said, lowering his voice. "I mean who are you in this hotel? You are doing everything as you were told. *Yes?* This is important."

"Absolutely. I am, for the present, Jurgen Enkert everywhere but at home. As for Jurgen Todt, he exists nowhere but in Bonn."

"Very good."

"And you switched the plates on your car? You are using the ones we gave you, and the rental registration. Correct?"

"Yes, yes."

"I see you've taken off your wedding ring."

"As instructed."

"And you have your new ID?"

"Of course."

Kreigsman took out a package of unfiltered Camels, put one in his mouth, and lit it.

"I'm not being impolite," he said. "I know you do not smoke. But you don't mind, do you? It does not bother you?"

They'd done this dance before. Jurgen did not know why Kreigsman bothered to ask now when he never had previously.

He sighed.

"Of course not."

Kreigsman took a long deep draw on the cigarette; then he exhaled an enormous draft of smoke, briefly turning his head away from Jurgen as he did so.

"These will accomplish what the ghouls at Auschwitz never could," he said, smiling. "These will kill me for sure."

Jurgen did not know what to say at the mention of Auschwitz.

"I'm sorry," he mumbled.

"It is alright. All is learning. Sometimes the best view of God is from Hell. I feel that."

Kreigsman put his cigarette down in an ashtray.

"And your father? He is well?"

"Not really. He is broken. He is a ghost waiting for the grave-diggers to arrive. He really might just as well have been hung."

"Trust me, I do not disagree. But how did he react to seeing you? Did he welcome you?"

"He welcomed me, but in the same way a corpse might greet guests at its own funeral."

"Did he come to trust you?"

"Yes. Quickly. Immediately. As if there was no question. He is too tired and uncaring – and, I suppose, unimportant – to be suspicious. Besides, I am his son."

"Did he confide anything of use?"

Jurgen nodded.

"Just a bit. Enough. The key thing is there does seem to be some small amount of support, a stipend of sorts, coming from where you'd suspected."

"This is no surprise. And the *brother*?"

Jurgen shook his head.

"He has no idea. Not the slightest notion. No contact."

"You are sure?"

"Yes."

"And so you are here."

"And so I am here."

"He took your suggestion? He made the request? You are representing him?"

Jurgen nodded.

"Damn good," said Kreigsman. "Damn good. May the small fish help us find the great shark."

The older man slapped Jurgen on the back.

"You are doing an excellent thing, my friend."

"Well, I am trying. We'll see."

"It will be fine. You are perfect for the job. You are a gift from God."

Jurgen shrugged.

"I'd really rather not be a gift from God. But as you three have convinced me, I suppose someone from my family owes something back. Someone with the name *Enkert* should make a gesture, an effort. And I am the only one."

The two men talked for nearly an hour. After they had finished several rounds, Kreigsman told him where he could be reached – at another hotel three miles away under the name *Gerber*.

"But now I'll leave you to rest. Try to relax to-night and tomorrow. Call your cute wife. Get a good night's sleep and refresh. I have something I've got to do here in town tomorrow morning. You take it easy while I work. Just be a tourist, and make your call to that bitch blonde Raff some time after lunch. Then let's meet here about this same time. OK?"

*

The man at the reception desk clearly tried not to look startled when Jurgen produced his identification. This was the very reason why for years, ever since his mother died, his tante had presented him to the world as *Todt*, Jurgen Todt – his mother's and his tante's maiden name. Jurgen found himself wondering whether this man who took his passport and credit card, and assigned him a room, was a Jew. He also found himself wondering whether or not he should say something – perhaps a convenient lie, such as: "I know what you're thinking. Just my luck, eh? No relation." But he didn't. There was no point. He simply took his key and headed for the elevator.

Jurgen tossed his bag onto the large bed in his well-appointed room. Then he looked out over the city from his tenth floor perch.

Cars and pedestrians moved in all directions. In the distance he could see the dark flow of the Spree. More closely there arose the enormous dome of St.

Hedwig's Cathedral, on the Bebelplatz – an ornate 18th century Church destroyed by air raids in 1943 and now rebuilt.

As Jurgen knew from the papers, the body of the Rev. Bernhard Lichtenberg – a cathedral canon who died on a train bound for Dachau after protesting conditions in concentration camps and praying publicly for the victims of Krystallnacht – had recently been recovered and interred in the crypt below the cathedral altar. Both a priest and a rabbi officiated at the services.

He realized he should be weary, but he wasn't. This was what happened to mild-mannered dealers of antiques and art when their boring but pleasant lives were suddenly up-heaved. It was funny how little it took to completely change one's world: just a few conversations with mysterious angels of righteousness, a visit to a father whom one had thought he'd never see again, and a long drive from Bonn to Munich, then on to Berlin. Now his entire reality stood redefined by just a few simple changes in the way of information, hours, and geography. Here he stood. No way of going-back. No way to erase any of it. For good or bad, nothing would ever be the same again.

He picked up the phone and quickly dialed his

home number. Ruth answered on the third ring.

"I knew it was *you*," she said. "I miss you. Eli misses you. Any luck?"

"Yes," he answered dryly. "A *wonderful* reunion."

"Such sarcasm. But really, I mean, he *is* your father."

"I either don't feel anything or I am secretly afraid to feel anything. For whatever reason, there's really nothing there. In a way I'm sorry that's the case; in a way I'm not. He does not seem to have learned anything, I'll tell you that. He's still a good Nazi. I think his head would explode if I ever told him about you and Eli."

"That's sad. I thought maybe things would be different. People *do* change you know."

"Not him."

"But it went well otherwise?"

"Yes. Just as planned. Just as hoped."

"So, what's next?"

"Now I've come to Berlin."

"Oh good. To see that woman?"

"Yes."

"Don't let her seduce you!" she joked. "I've seen the pictures!"

"Have no fear. The very thought makes me want to take a shower."

"Good! I'll take care of you when you get back here!"

He pictured her pouty smirk on the other end of the line, and then – he could not help himself – conjured the image of her naked, in their bed, inviting him.

"Alright. Love you."

*

Early the next morning, Kreigsman sat on a park bench on the northern end of Berlin's beautiful and wooded Tiergarten, not far from where the park bordered the banks of the Spree. He had a job to do today, as did the gypsy Harman, so far away.

Kreigsman appeared to all the world like the most innocent and benign of beings. He held a bag of bird-seed in his hands. He smiled as he tossed the stuff out to a gathering batch of pigeons. Two young girls in short dresses strolled by; Kreigsman enjoyed the view. Two boys tossed a frisbee back and forth on the lawn some distance away, while others practiced kicking balls at a net. "You can do better than that!" shouted the guard who stood before the net. "Knock it past me! Go ahead. Go for the goal!" *Yes*, thought Kreigsman. *Go for the goal.*

He'd been at the bench for about half an hour when the man he expected finally arrived. The man looked about ten years older than Kreigsman, and seemed not in nearly as good shape. He walked slowly, with a cane, and showed the general dishevelment frequently displayed by men somewhat tired of the world: conventional souls who, in their dotage, have decided either consciously or unconsciously to let the conventions slip a bit. He wore a suit, but it was wrinkled and needed a washing. On his feet he wore a completely out-of-place pair of white sneakers. His tie bore a mustard stain. He needed a shave. His gray hair had apparently not been combed in recent memory.

As he approached the bench he smiled broadly.

"Didn't you see my invisible sign?" he joked. "This is my bench. These are my pigeons."

"Apologies," Kreigsman answered. "Perhaps, just for today, we might share them, both the bench and the birds?"

"Alright," said the man, sitting down beside him. "But if you come back tomorrow you'll have to get your own!"

"Who knows if either of us will come back to-morrow?"

"A good point. One can only hope and pray!"

The man took a bag of seed from his pocket and proceeded to join Kreigsman in feeding the birds.

"Some people say they are nothing but rats," said the man. "But I don't know. For some reason I love them. They are just trying to make their way, after all."

"I take it you come here often."

The man nodded.

"Every day. I am very boring and predictable, I'm afraid. But I've never seen you before."

"No. I'm from out of town. Vienna. Only here for a few days."

"Pleasure?"

"No. Business."

"I used to be in business. Now I am retired. I'm not sure it was a good idea to retire. Once you quit you start to let yourself go. You lose discipline. But, at the same time, I wouldn't go back."

"What did you do?"

"Accountant. A long life of numbers. Nothing but balance sheets, and bank slips. A long life of counting things."

"Oh, I see. I was never much good with numbers. Not my *forte*."

"And what is your *forte*?"

"I come from a family of chemists. You know, pharmacists."

"Agh. A family tradition. A professional family tradition. That's nice."

"Indeed," said Kreigsman.

"Your father? And then his father before him?"

"Actually, yes."

"And you are still active in this?"

"Sometimes," Kreigsman answered.

Upon saying this, Kreigsman reached into his pocket, produced a syringe, and plunged it into the man's leg. Almost instantly, the man went limp, his eyes wide and his mouth open. He dropped the bag of seed into his lap.

Kreigsman knew he could still hear.

"Pancuronium bromide," he said matter-of-factly. "It paralyzes all the muscles. Even the respiratory muscles. You will asphyxiate very shortly. By the way, several of the corpses you counted at Auschwitz belonged to my family. Goodbye."

Kreigsman drew out a folded sheet of paper and placed it in the man's breast pocket. Then he emptied what was left from both bags of seed onto what would shortly be a corpse.

Kreigsman calmly strolled away. Behind him, the birds flocked upon the motionless body in a mad frenzy of feeding.

*

With his back turned to the priest who sat near the desk, Kolm stood and looked out the large window of his office. He gazed past the spire of the Catholic Church of St. Benedict, and across the rooftops of Bayreuth to the the Bavarian countryside beyond: fertile green fields, deep forests, the grand Fichelgebirge Mountains, and the beautiful Red Main. Finally set loose from its confining concrete channel here in the city center, the flowing water rushed eagerly through the valley towards its junction with the Main.

He could see the peak of the Bayreuth Festspielehaus, designed by the great Richard Wagner himself, where for generations the master's operas – so vital as rites of secular nationalism and Nordic self-realization – had been performed.

The Führer had been quite correct to extoll Wagner as the embodiment of German culture. Ancient emblems, as well as heroic themes of purity and destiny, ran through the composer's works – all of them imbued with Teutonic glory.

Such a genius was that man Wagner. And what insight! As early as 1850 he'd written to warn against the influence of Judaism in the arts. Whenever the Jew produced music or images or literature, observed Wagner, his ambition was not to create great, soaring eternal works, but rather to gather shallow popularity and financial gain. Of course Wagner was right. The Jew seemed incapable of majesty, because he had not the character to achieve it.

Kolm had always loved to immerse himself in the cathartic rituals which lay at the heart of Wagner's most triumphant works. This was no small reason why he'd made Bayreuth his home all these years. The performances at the Festspielehaus always re-newed Kolm's energy, not to mention his faith that this long winter of defeat would one day end and Germany's true destiny of dominion be fulfilled.

Kolm's office occupied most of the mansion's attic space. The paintings on the walls included several nudes displaying the perfection of pure Aryan womanhood, all of these by Adolf Ziegler, the same artist whom Adolph Hitler himself had long ago tasked to purge Germany of degenerate art. As Chairman of the Reich Chamber for Visual Arts, Ziegler had proved himself to be quite dedicated. He zealously suppressed the chaos of the avant-garde and expressionist styles in favor of Romantic realism and traditional, classical approaches. Kolm as well cherished several genre paintings by Adolf Wissel (another Hitler favorite), these showing idealized rural farm life in the German countryside: the world as it ought to be, at least for most simple souls.

Along with these images hung a succession of landscape photographs taken by Kolm himself. Here were all the great Black Forest peaks: Feldberg, Herzogenhorn, Belchen, Kandel. Not just a vigorous mountaineer but also an amateur photographer and naturalist, Kolm considered himself something of an expert on the geology, hydrology, wildlife, flora, and fauna of that particular region: his natal place.

But as it was, regardless of his many journeys back to scale those wondrous summits, he'd always made it a point to avoid his hometown of Altensteig and the countryside immediately surrounding the village. Indeed, his secret lodge – owned under yet another alias, one known only to himself – stood nowhere near Altensteig. After all, chance encounters would not be good. Old acquaintances and cousins had to be avoided and left with the presumption of his death. This was the only safe course of action.

Kolm's desk, before which the priest sat, was an ornate affair. Carved and cobbled from the finest German oak more than a century before, the piece had once been owned by the Grand Duke of Hesse, brother to the tragic last Tsarina of Imperial Russia. Across its leather top lay a bit of correspondence and a neat pile of dossiers. Kolm's file cabinets stood at rigid attention in strict military order on the far side of the room, their contents meticulously referenced and counter-referenced – immaculately arranged.

Kolm's phone rang with what he supposed was the call he and the priest had been waiting for.

"It is Albert Steiner calling from Berlin," said the woman, Ingrid, who served variously as Kolm's receptionist, hostess, assistant, and lover – each of these tasks executed in the most efficient, practical, and professional of manners. (Kolm confined his romantic notions to nation, music, art, and nature. Whatever remaining slim shard of sentiment he possessed did not extend to sexual relations.)

"Shall I put him through?"

"By all means," Kolm answered.

"*Guten tag,* Heinz," said the voice on the other end of the line.

"*Guten tag,* Albert. I am putting you on speaker phone as the Confessor is here. How is Berlin?"

"I'm afraid no better than usual. Increasingly bourgeois and boring."

"Sometimes I think you are even more of a snob than I am!"

"How could that even be possible?" the voice on the other end of the line chided.

"Only with much effort. Well, what news do you have for us?"

"I've thought it over carefully. I've studied the plan backwards and forwards. I'm impressed with the organization and the careful attention to detail – although I suppose I should not have expected anything other than that from our friend. So, the Confessor's Bonn project has my blessing. Go ahead. Do it up grand. Make it very loud. Send a clear message. It's what that traitor Brandt deserves if he seriously thinks of selling tanks to Israel."

"Wonderful!" said the priest, speaking for the first time. "I'm so glad you've come to see things my way."

"You have the men in place?"

"Yes," answered the priest. "All is ready. Everything rehearsed. A very quick in and out. It will be
over almost before it begins. And I will of course be
there myself, in command."

The priest – whom the few comrades who knew
him called the *Confessor* – looked to be about the same
age as Kolm. Closely cropped gray hair circled the
bald dome of his head. A hideous blue and black
stain, this being a birthmark, covered half his face.
His eyes – alert but cold – shown deep blue.

"Then, my friends" said Albert, "I shall leave you
to it."

Kolm hung up the receiver.

"A drink?" he asked the Confessor.

"Certainly."

Kolm went to a sideboard. He poured two glasses
of sherry. Returning and handing one to the priest, he
proposed a toast.

"To success," he said.

"*Yes!*" echoed the priest. "To success!"

The Confessor looked forward to doing good
work very soon. A true day of atonement. A Yom
Kippur not to be forgotten.

*

Not far from where Kreigsman encountered and dealt with his prey, Jurgen browsed the streets. He followed instructions. He acted the tourist. Which in fact he was.

He wandered past the many shops of the Bebelplatz, not far from his hotel. He stopped at a bakery for a roll and coffee. Then he continued on down to the doors of St. Hedwig's, just as he'd known he would. A longtime student of art and architecture, as well as a devout Catholic, Jurgen always found such places fascinating.

He thought it ironic that the dome and many other design elements of Hedwig's – its foundation stone, according to the plaque out front, laid in 1747 – had been inspired by the Pantheon in Rome, just as were several of Speer's more fantastical architectural schemes.

Upon entering, Jurgen found himself in total and immediate awe of the church's great beauty. A late Gothic Marian figure stared down at all who entered. Grand, ornate tapestries hung on the walls, pre-senting themes from the Book of Revelation. A mas-sive gold cross floated above the main altar. He took a seat in a pew facing the cross and, ignoring the flash-bulbs and loud whispers of the tourists, knelt to pray.

But he did not stay long. One *Lord's Prayer*, one *Hail Mary*, one *Act of Contrition*. Then he was on his way.

Upon leaving the church, Jurgen walked in the direction of the Brandenburg Gate, just to the west of the Pariser Platz, at the intersection of Unter den Linden and Ebertstrasse and only a block away from the Reichtag. Jurgen marveled at the enormous 18th century arch's grand neoclassical lines. How ironic that when first constructed the arch had been called *Friedenstor*, Gate of Peace. The ornate Quadriga statue atop – Victory driving a chariot – had for nearly two centuries faced east. But once the Russians built the wall, the leaders of the Federal Republic pointedly turned the statue to face the other direction. Jurgen looked on as his fellow Germans somberly passed through the checkpoint between East and West.

Jurgen knew that not far from the eastern side of the Gate lay the grim remains of Albert Speer's grand Reich Chancellery (not just the famous bunker, but much of the lower Chancellery itself). There the once grand rooms brooded darkly, long ago bull-dozed over, a haunting and cavernous amalgamation of lost frescoes and endless corridors – all of this far beyond the reach of the general public, but sometimes accessible by those with both curiosity and contacts. Those who visited described a vast tomb housing nothing but the gnarled corpse of grand ambition. One such privileged interloper told him the once fanatically polished tile floors now hosted vast fields of mildew.

From the Gate, Jurgen walked the long street which ran from the center of the Tiergarten to the great oval structure of the Olympic Stadium, its giant pillars of pale stone providing sparse decoration atop of an over-riding motif of stark, druidical simplicity. Stepping inside the arena, Jurgen imagined he could hear the cheers of spectators, and see the grim ghost of Adolf Hitler standing on high.

Later on, he stopped in several antique shops to see what was about in the way of merchandise, and what prices were fetched (or, at least, *sought*). The "homework" of an art and antiques dealer never ended. Values and prices ebbed and flowed constantly, along with fads and fashions. One period or style outranked another for a few years, then the situation flipped completely on some undiagnosed, random tic of the market. One had to keep his hand on the pulse of things. Otherwise it was very easy to go broke.

He loved it though. The quality, craftsmanship, and *spirit* of "old" things. Objects which defied the modern. Objects which carried echoes of generations long passed away. Objects which spoke to tradition and heritage and, at least in an abbreviated way, suggested the constancy of the eternal. After all, in religious terms – the only terms which really, in the final analysis, meant anything to him – the "now" of this world was quite a drawn-out affair embracing all of mortal past, present, and future. A blink of God's eye. *We break bread with the dead,* he thought, *every day in nearly every way.*

Walking down Pestalozzi Strasse in the Charlottenburg district, he spotted a beautiful turn-of-the-century synagogue tucked away in a small courtyard. It stood in the Romanesque style, but also featured the all-brick exterior and looming proportions routinely exhibited in traditional medieval German structures. Jurgen found such combinations interesting. Curious, he entered. He was glad to find a box of yarmulkes in the lobby. He put one on before proceeding further. As he did so, he was approached by an elderly, shaggy-bearded man wearing an equally-old suit and a prayer shawl.

"*Guten tag,*" said the man. "And may I help you?"

"I don't mean to intrude, but I was hoping I might look around a bit."

"You are very welcome. I thought I was right. I

thought I did not recognize you."

"No. I am not from here. I am from Bonn." Then, after a pause: "And I am not Jewish."

The old man chuckled.

"Don't be ashamed. Many people are from Bonn, though few admit it. *And even more people are not Jews, believe it or not!* But no one is perfect. Now come in. Let me show you what you are missing. My name is Peter Levi, by the way."

"And I am Jurgen."

"I'm sure you are."

The old man took him by the arm, leading him through a large set of brass doors, into the sanctuary – a beautiful space of superb classical lines, its walls featuring intricately-carved woodwork. Jurgen left no corner of the place uninspected. The old man allowed him all the time he needed to take it in, and answered many questions.

"So beautiful. One does not see many pre-war synagogues so well preserved as this," Jurgen exclaimed.

"Sadly, no. In fact, this synagogue itself nearly did not survive. The Brownshirts set it on fire during Kristallnacht, but then their superiors ordered the blaze extinguished to protect some neighboring buildings and homes they wanted to preserve. Of course, then they confiscated and closed the place. But now we're here and they're not."

"I'm so glad it still stands."

The old man nodded.

"I watched the whole thing. I lived in a building across the street. From six floors up I watched the mob come with their torches and clubs. I saw them rush the courtyard and knock down the doors. A house of God! A place of peace! Who could believe it? Honestly, I never thought things would go so far. We were German Jews, after all. *German* Jews. I am a very old man. I have, or at least I *had*, an Iron Cross from the Great War. So, I am a decorated veteran, yes? For this reason, I thought, never will me or mine have a serious problem. Then one day I wore my medal out on my walk, along with my required Star of David, as if the medal might serve as some sort of talisman to protect me. You know what happened? A boy who looked not yet 15, a *child* wearing a Hitler Youth uniform, walked up and ripped it off my chest. He did not say a word. Just walked away with it. But such hate in his eyes. Then I knew. *Then I knew*."

"So many stories," Jurgen said. "I was just a small boy then. I can't imagine."

"It is hard to understand if you did not experience it. But don't worry. I won't burden you with my autobiography. It is the same one you have heard already, by the hundreds. And besides, I am tired of telling it."

"My wife is Jewish," Jurgen volunteered quite spontaneously. "She lost both her parents."

"And you've already admitted you are not Jewish."

"No. Catholic."

"Agh. Well, once again, don't feel too badly. At least you married well."

Jurgen found the old man's dry humor – this full of hard-to-understand joy merged with what was obviously very profound wisdom – quite endearing. Peter Levi, it seemed, was one of those people you could not know for more than five minutes without coming to love.

"So," Levi said, leading him to the exit, "now you have seen what you came to see. I will tell you something. This was once an Orthodox synagogue before the Nazis, but now we are quite liberal. We even have an organ and choir. We might as well be Lutherans! But I like it."

Once they were back in the lobby, Jurgen returned his yarmulke to the box and shook Peter Levi's
hand in thanks. He would never see Peter Levi again;
but he would also never forget him.

*

Harman walked down the principal dock at
Hamburg's City Sporthaven, just off the Vorsetzen,
near where the highway and the parallel Elbe met
Binnenhafen and the Zollkanal. The city, which he
hated – but then he hated most cities – roared behind
him in the busy afternoon.

He'd been hungry when he arrived two hours
before, but could only find grotesquely highly-priced
eateries. Such was the neighborhood. He'd have to
talk to Kreigsman about that. Parking had proved
another expensive proposition. He was not a rich
man. He'd need some reimbursement. He'd been
careful to keep his receipts in case he was not believed – a hazard of reputation (ethnic reputation,
rather than personal). A hazard with which he was
used to dealing.

He eyed the long dock – a jewelry chain from
which dangled the most beautiful and expensive of
boats large and small: ostentatious personal cruisers,

immaculate sailboats, and even a few houseboats, each made fast with thick lines wrapped around pilings. People lounged or did busy work on a few of them, but most of the vessels seemed quite empty on this weekday.

Harman was not a man of the waterfront, so the atmosphere of this place was new to him, and interesting. The Elbe danced blue under a clear sky. The river stood high, the North Sea in its eternal rhythm having just flooded inland an hour before. Now the Elbe waited expectantly, calmly, for the ebb to begin.

Ravenous gulls descended in groups to fight over odd scraps of food laying here and there. Large commercial tankers and freighters – the *real* residents of these waters, this busy industrial port and harbor – trudged slowly up and down, south and north, the noise of their engines and blasts of their horns rising to form a fevered cacophony.

No one took much notice of Harman as he casually continued down the dock to its very end, and he was glad.

He saw the black-hulled schooner, with the name *Barbarossa* in gold lettering at the bow, just where the dock-master, in his tiny office at the top of the pier, had said she'd be.

"You a friend of Wolfgang's?" the man had asked.

"Something like that."

"Well, he's *in residence,* as they say. Been living aboard for a week. He does that every now and then. Maintenance, you know. It's a bitch."

"Indeed. Well, good. Thank you."

As Harman approached he spotted Wolfgang in the cockpit, busily applying a coat of varnish to the long tiller. A stiff breeze blew off the river. Nevertheless, Wolfgang Kleug worked bare-chested, in shorts, barefoot.

Harman stood at the brink of the dock. He took in the vessel admiringly: the beautiful and inexplicable complexity of the rigging (if that was the term – he thought so, probably), the precise neatness of the carefully coiled lines on deck, the immaculate dinghy (or was it a lifeboat?) hanging from the stern, and the host of obtuse pulleys, wenches, and other gear which glistened everywhere.

One thing for sure: this was no poor man's plaything.

It did not take long for Wolfgang to notice him.

"*Guten tag!*" he shouted. "You like what you see?"

"Yes. She is very beautiful! Amazing, really."

"You sail?"

"No, no. I'm really just a tourist when it comes to these things. *A voyeur*, you might say. I could not tell starboard from port if my life depended on it. In fact, I've never been on the water even once in my life, if you can believe that. But I love the artistry of these vessels. The joy for me is just to look at them."

"You don't know what you are missing," said Wolfgang, putting his brush down on a sheet of newspaper. "You should try it sometime. A young man like you. You have no idea how splendid it can be out there with the wind and water."

Harman laughed.

"A young man like me? Thank you for the compliment. I am forty!"

"Well, I am over seventy, so you are young to me! Say, would you like a tour? I love to show her off."

"How kind. I've always been curious. *Danka*!"

"Step aboard! I am Wolfgang."

"And I am Harman."

"Harman? That is an interesting name. I've never heard it."

"Where I come from it means a hardy, bold man."

The tide being high, the schooner floated nearly level with the dock, so it really was just a "step" to get aboard, whereas he might otherwise have had to jump down several feet.

Wolfgang spent a solid hour or more walking Harman about the deck, giving him great detail – actually, *too much* detail – about objects Wolfgang referred to variously as spars, booms, and jibs. Then, pointing high above, he explained a dozen or so additional tools, devices, and features: the topmast, topsail yard, lower yard, main gaff, and fore gaff. Harman's head swam with the information, only a fraction of which he was able to retain.

"Might I see below?" Harman asked eventually. "I don't mean to intrude."

"Of course! I was just getting to that. Come!"

Wolfgang led Harman to the cockpit and then through a hatch and down a slanted ladder into a beautiful and comfortable space. To the left Harman saw the galley, to the right a small desk built into the hull, a desk on which sat what looked like navigational equipment and a radio.

"The engine room is behind us," said Wolfgang. "Up here is the main saloon."

They stepped through a companion-way into a spacious room. In one corner stood a rectangular eating table surrounded by a curved bench, this providing seating on three sides. Across from that stood a door to what Wolfgang called the "captain's cabin, where I hang my hat!" The cabin included a double-sized bunk and built-in drawers.

Beyond the saloon, through another companion-way, one found two sets of double bunks on the starboard and port sides, and beyond these two heads similarly situated, with a second set of steep steps leading up to to the fore-deck. Finally, at the rapidly narrowing bow, Wolfgang pointed to another door which he identified as the rope-locker.

"But come back to the saloon with me," said Wolfgang. "Let's have a beer."

Once in the saloon, Wolfgang indicated Harman should take a seat at the table. Wolfgang went to a refrigerator in the galley where he retrieved two cold bottles of a good local brew.

"We get our electric for the fridge, lights, and radio from the marina while we're in port," Wolfgang volunteered, setting the opened bottles down on the table. "At sea we have several batteries which we can recharge with the diesel engine."

"This is the life," said Harman. "To you!"

Harman raised his beer; he and Wolfgang tapped bottles.

"You have an interesting accent," said Wolfgang. "You speak German well, but I can tell it is not your native tongue."

"No, not really, though I've spoken German most of my life."

"And what is your native tongue?"

"Romani."

"Romani? Like the Gypsies?"

"As a matter of fact, yes. You're quite right. Exactly like the Gypsies."

As he said this, Harman drew a .38 with a silencer from the shoulder-holster underneath his jacket and fired a bullet point-blank into Wolfgang's forehead. Wolfgang collapsed face down on the table. Harman reached into his pocket and pulled out a note. The note claimed credit for the execution and explained why it had occurred. He placed this on the table beneath a glass ashtray.

No one looked at him twice as he walked back up the dock.

Chapter 2

It had all started so benignly back in April, and in the least likely of places: an antiques auction just a bit to the south of Bonn, in the suburb of Bad Godesberg. Jurgen had been drawn to the event through a catalogue which featured a 19th-century Bavarian armoire he knew he could export for a good price, also a late 18th-century baroque style desk he believed he could easily "turn" through dealers in either New York or London.

When he arrived at the auction hall he spotted the two pieces he coveted. They had high lot numbers, which meant they'd be among the last items to go on the block. Sighing, he braced himself for a long evening of jewelry and silver services and paintings before the affair would finally wind down to the two pieces he sought. Never mind. It was all just a part of the job. Besides, he always found it interesting to see what different items went for. One could never have too much knowledge.

Jurgen placed his jacket and bid-card on a seat, to hold it, then went to inspect the armoire and desk. Carefully, and with the precision of a true expert, he studied their tops and bottoms and sides, took critical looks at their joints, and examined their cabinetry. He scrutinized the dovetailing of the wood, the variances of the boards front and back, and the age and condition of the locks and other hardware.

The Bavarian armoire seemed to have been built by an anonymous craftsman, albeit a highly skilled one. The desk, he was sure, came from Hamburg's Ernest Bruck – a distinguished 18th century woodworker whose pieces were scarce and much sought after by collectors. Bruck's work could be easily identified by tell-tale signs which plainly revealed themselves to trained eyes. Thus Jurgen prayed for a scarcity of trained eyes.

It was good the catalogue did not mention Bruck. Some employee of the auction house had been slack in doing his or her homework. Jurgen only hoped any competing bidders might be just as ignorant. Sometimes luck like that could strike. And a Bruck would easily sell for five times the price of the same item from some other, or an unknown, maker. Jurgen tried not to look pleased or excited as he walked back to his chair.

A beefy bald man in a wrinkled suit occupied the seat beside him, previously empty. The hall was hot.

The man fanned himself with the auction catalogue. He smiled and nodded as Jurgen sat down.

"This is my first auction," said the man. "I don't know a damned thing about this stuff."

"It can be fun," Jurgen answered.

"I put a few things up for sale. We'll see how they do."

"Cleaning out?"

"Yes. Some junk from the attic. Lots more of it to go, sad to say. The home of an old aunt who has gone to God. Old family home."

"Here in town?"

"Yes. Just three streets over. I am camped out for the time being, until I empty the place. I'm from Lichtenau."

Jurgen, sensed an opportunity.

"You know. I am a dealer. I make a small specialty of estates – clearing out estates. Buying. I can buy all or some of it from you if we can agree on a price. Or I can just give you appraisals for a small fee. If you would like me to come by it is no problem. I am only in Bonn."

"That sounds interesting. Do you have a card?"

Jurgen produced his card.

"My wife is from your part of the country," Jurgen volunteered. "From Alsace. In fact another part of Baden-Württemberg. Stuttgart. Her parents are Schroeder."

The man thought for a moment, then shook his head.

"I know no Schroeders. But that is a very common name. Also, Stuttgart is a whole different world from quiet Lichtenau. I rarely get there. Baden-Württemberg is a far bigger place than many people imagine."

The man raised Jurgen's business card and studied it.

"Thank you for this. I will definitely call you. My name is Rubin, by the way."

The auction dragged on forever. Rubin left halfway through the evening, evidently after his lots had come up. He'd not indicated which items were his. Standing to leave, he patted Jurgen on the shoulder and whispered: "We'll talk soon."

Jurgen found himself outbid for the armoire, but managed to get the Bruck – which no-one else appeared to have recognized. Thus he acquired the piece at what he considered a bargain price. He was sure he'd be able to at least triple his money, and do so without much effort, making a profit of several thousand. A good month's work, he told himself, done all in one evening. If only he could have more such windfalls.

When he finally got back home he found Ruth sound asleep, with three-year-old Eli close beside her in bed. This was not a regular event. He thought the boy must have had a nightmare.

Before Jurgen joined them he sat in the living room for a few minutes and decompressed. He drank a half-litre mug of good beer and watched the late television news. The news held nothing remarkable or of particular interest. Near Bremen, investigators had discovered a previously unknown Nazi-era stash of looted paintings and sculptures. More than a thousand objects filled an obscure bunker. Government conservators were busy removing the pieces and taking them to be catalogued, after which the rightful owners – some of them hopefully still alive – or their heirs would be sought. Elsewhere, Chancellor Willie Brandt continued to suffer attacks – *deserved* attacks, Jurgen thought – for supporting Richard Nixon's ridiculous continuation of the absurd U.S. war in Vietnam.

Jurgen finished his beer. When at last he climbed

into bed, his son turned and curled up around him, murmuring calm indecipherable words out of the depths of his sleep.

*

When Jurgen first met Ruth, he'd not known what to say – or, frankly, whether to seek or hide. She was the most beautiful woman he had ever encountered, with long brown hair, exquisite gray eyes, a thin face, and a perfect body. She was, as well, articulate, intelligent, and – *miraculously, wonderfully* – drawn to him. ("I can't help it," she'd laughed on their second date. "I just can't resist you blonde Aryan supermen." Then she'd kissed him, making the first move, giving him no choice but to need her all the more.)

But that, Jurgen knew, was just the problem. Jurgen did indeed represent the classic blonde Aryan superman – but in more ways than Ruth realized. Even before he understood her history, when all he knew for sure was that she was a Jew, he wondered how she could ever accept, let alone desire, someone with his associations and background – his dark pedigree. He feared that if she knew she would surely find him repellent. He feared, if she possessed the truth, she would most certainly curse him and all of his blood. After all, even in his own mind and opinion he reeked with the foul odor of his origins. Not just his Nazi father and mother, but all of it.

It was Lisel who told him not to think that way. The truth of the past was *not* something he should allow to influence his definition of himself. "You are no more guilty by your blood," she told him, "than all those poor six million Jews were guilty by their blood. They were innocent, yes. But so are *you* innocent. The sins of those who came before you *are not your sins.* Why should you be punished? Why should you be denied love? And why should Ruth be denied love?"

Lisel told him she had not worked so hard to bury the past just so he could be haunted by its ghost. She'd labored to set him free, and he owed her that: *to be free.* The truth, when he finally told it, ran over Ruth like water. "They are not you," she said, referring to his parents. "There is no shame for you."

They dated throughout their sophomore year at Universität Bonn and then – much to Lisel's Catholic distress, even though she had come to love Ruth and believed profoundly the two young people belonged together – took an apartment without benefit of marriage. The couple did not wed until after their graduations – she with her degree is journalism and documentary film, he with his in art and architecture.

They married in the synagogue. Jurgen pledged any children would be raised in their mother's faith. Then Eli came. And always ever since they'd had bliss, happiness, and honesty – though they rarely discussed the past, at least not Ruth's past. It was clearly not a topic Ruth wanted to dwell upon, not even during the several times of year when they'd visit her step-parents at the home in which she'd been raised. In fact, Jurgen had never gotten anything but the barest bones of her story from Ruth herself. It was her step-father, Wilfried, who'd been candid.

Jurgen remembered one day sitting in Wilfried's office in the economics department at the Universität Stuttgart, the two of them alone, as Wilfried spun the tale. He explained how Ruth's parents, childhood friends of Wilfried and Margaret, had come from the hinterlands one late, dark night, without prior notice, carrying their little girl, who already knew Wilfried and Margaret as her beloved, though honorary, uncle and aunt. He recalled how the couple, afraid they would be taken for relocation any day, begged for shelter for their child. He described how he and Margaret freely and immediately acquiesced, believing the interlude would be temporary, just as the Reich was bound to be. And he told of how the parents, named Wurtz, never returned.

"He was a dentist," said Wilfried. "At least until he was no longer permitted to practice. She was a housewife, and a wonderfully talented pianist. She gave lessons to children in her home, although that too ended."

"And they themselves ended at Treblinka?"

Wilfried nodded.

"This is what the Red Cross told us. Not gassed. They appear nowhere on the manifest for gassing. But we believe they went there, along with all the other Jews from that neighborhood. And we know they never came back. Perhaps medical experiments. Or just plain starvation. Still, all will be well. With God there is inevitable judgment and justice, Jurgen. If not in this life, in the next."

Jurgen had a great affection for both Wilfried and Margaret, but especially for Wilfried. After all, he'd grown up without a father. Once Jurgen and Ruth got together, Wilfried became something of a surrogate. Jurgen admired the man – his uprightness, his uncompromising ethics, his charity, and most of all his modesty. Who would guess the rumpled, diminutive, pipe-smoking fellow who held happy Eli by the hand and walked him to the playground had authored more than 20 seminal treatises on international trade, and stood as one of the most prominent scholars in his field, both at home and abroad?

Jurgen and Wilfried could spend hours talking politics and history and art. Through the years, they came to know each other's minds very well. Sitting in his chair in the living room in Stuttgart, his pipe lit and the smoke rising, Wilfried (as Ruth said more than once, *always the teacher*) effortlessly wove facts into narratives and narratives into lessons – lessons disguised as stories. Thus Wilfried routinely increas-ed one's intellectual understanding – but always in the most humane, quiet, and artful manner. With his broad, eclectic learning, and his devout faith, Wilfried seemed Catholic in more ways than one – in a manner embracing both the small and the capital C. Wilfried was the same way with Eli. More than once Jurgen heard *Papa Wilfried* utter the phrase: "Now let me tell you a story ..."

Jurgen thought stories to be the most powerful of things. This was especially the case with true stories, because they were inescapable and never went away. Even when never spoken or written, they still lingered – eternal, undeniable, containing variously either blessings or curses. The stories Wilfried told Eli were uniformly of the former type, full of magic and light and revelation. No rush, thought Jurgen, for the boy to encounter all those *other* stories – the ones which loitered down the darkest alleys of memory – the ones full of doubt and shame.

*

Two days following his first encounter with Rubin, after a brief phone call, Jurgen pulled the van he used for business up in front of a rustic alpine-style house in a quiet neighborhood of Bad Godesberg.

From a distance, the place seemed almost overly picturesque – as if it might have been built from gingerbread and might be home to a merry band of lederhosen-wearing elves.

Children kicked a ball down the street, boisterously enjoying the spring weather after a hard, white winter. An old woman, bundled up in an overcoat despite the warmth, walked her dog in the direction of the northern avenue. She paused now and then as the pup stopped to make his mark of ownership on various trees and hydrants. While walking along she mumbled, either to herself or to her dog. Her gait was slow, measured, and just the tiniest bit unsteady. It provided a strangely appropriate counterpoint to the frantic syncopation of the kids with their shouts and their ball. As he stepped from his van, Jurgen heard the bell of a nearby medieval church toll the time of ten AM. The sound bore the authority of age and grace – a message of tradition and order.

The brass knocker beside the door felt heavy and uncompromising. Jurgen pounded twice. Each time he could hear the loud impact echoing down the interior hall.

It took a moment for Rubin to appear, shambling down the hall, all the while waving a hand to Jurgen through the glass. Then it took him a good minute or so to fumble with several dead-bolts.

"You found the place no problem!" he said as Jurgen entered.

He patted the young man on the arm and then turned his attention back to the dead-bolts, methodically throwing each one.

"And you are prompt! A sign of respect for other people's time. Always admirable. I like that. Such things are important, and all too rare these days."

Rubin led Jurgen back down the hall to the rear of the house.

They passed several large rooms on the way – one obviously the living room, another the dining room. Ornate fireplaces formed the centers of each. These were made even more prominent by the absence of much anything else in the way of furnishings. The living room held neither couches nor chairs nor tables – just two modern metal desks, each piled so high with papers and file folders there was no place to work at them. The dining room held neither table nor seats nor credenza, just a row of unlovely steel file cabinets lined up like soldiers. All the walls of both rooms, just like the walls of the hallway, stood completely devoid of ornament – no pictures, no clocks, no mirrors, no crucifixes. Nothing.

"And here is my lair!" Rubin said proudly. They entered a very small glassed-in conservatory/solarium overlooking a nice sized yard, the latter showing a delightful array of yellow, green, red, and magenta in its signaling of a ripe spring.

A desk almost too large for the space took up one end of the solarium. Rubin moved behind the desk and sat down, gesturing for Jurgen to take one of three other seats. A chair to the far right was already occupied.

"This is my friend Kreigsman. Jules Kreigsman. Say *hello* Jules."

Jules did not say hello. He simply shook Jurgen's hand while puffing on a cigarette.

"Don't call me *Jules*," he said. He removed the cigarette, all the while eyeing Jurgen with the quiet, skeptical, suspicious curiosity one might normally reserve for an unwanted door-to-door salesman. "Just call me *Kreigsman*."

Jurgen took a moment to look around the room. Aside from Rubin's desk – which actually looked old and interesting – he saw nothing worthwhile.

"Do you like all my antiques?" Rubin asked, smiling widely.

"I don't know. Where are they? Upstairs?"

"No. Sorry. The second and third floors hold nothing you'd find of interest. Some cots and television sets, a pool table, a few bookshelves ... mostly with paperback mysteries. Real trash."

Kreigsman and Rubin both chuckled. Jurgen did not.

"Then excuse me, but what exactly am I doing here?"

"I apologize," said Rubin. "Clearly you have been lured under false pretences."

Jurgen did not like the sound of the word *lured*.

"I suppose I certainly have been. What's going on?"

He grew angry. He'd rescheduled another potentially lucrative appointment to make time for this man Rubin. He was not amused, especially since he sensed Rubin and Kreigsman *were* amused.

"Relax," said Rubin. "Calm down. We bring you good news, Mr. Enkert."

Enkert? Jurgen was caught short, baffled. He did not know quite how to respond.

"Why," he asked, "do you call me that?"

"Because it is your name, is it not?" said Rubin.

"My name is ..."

"Yes, I know. *Todt*. Look, I understand. Mr. Kreigsman understands. OK? Do you hear what I'm saying? Things become necessary over time, in order to have a life. *We get it,* as the Americans would say. So ... Todt, Enkert, whatever. We know what we know. And trust me, we mean you no trouble. *None.*"

"Then what's this about?"

"Your father, Mr. Enkert."

"My father is dead," he said. "Or as good as dead. Either above-ground in some jungle or below-ground in some jungle. And if you think I have any idea where he is, you're wrong."

"We bring you tidings of great joy," Kreigsman said dryly. "Peter Enkert is very much above-ground."

"You are sure of this?"

"Quite sure."

Jurgen rolled his eyes. He really didn't care. The man was nothing more than an abstraction to him, and a grotesque: a figment of the past – a past he was not interested in reviving.

"Alright then. So he is alive. But what does it matter, and why do you tell me?"

"Because he will soon be returning to Germany."

"What? From where?"

"Probably from that jungle you just referred to, not that it matters. He's quite sick, dying in fact, and plans on coming home to do it."

"Who told you this?"

"It is not important," said Rubin. "We have our sources. The main thing is: we know."

"Are you *friends* of his? How are you connected here?"

Rubin and Kreigsman exchanged a glance and cracked smiles. Then Rubin answered.

"We are, what you might call *interested parties*."

"Listen, you two. I am not sure I want to continue this conversation."

Rubin nodded.

"I know. I understand. You do not trust us. And why should you? We started off by lying, right? We did that to get you here. You think us somehow sinister. You wonder if we are soldiers for a defeated cause, soldiers carrying on in the shadows. And if so, you do not wish to spend a single moment longer in our company, because you are not like us and you are *proud* not to be like us. You think in a different way. You are disgusted by what those of your blood have done in the past. You are ashamed! How could you not be, after all, when you are married to a Jew and have a son who is a Jew."

"What are you saying?"

"Nothing! Nothing besides the truth. Relax. As, I said at the start, we mean you no trouble. *None.*"

Jurgen did not respond.

"But still you do not trust us," said Rubin.

"I don't know what to think."

"Alright, hold on."

Rubin pushed a button on what looked to be an intercom.

"We are ready for you now," he said.

Then he looked at Jurgen and pointed to the ceiling.

"A colleague. Upstairs. He'll be here in a moment and he will be able to put your mind at ease. After that, we'll start to talk about serious matters."

    *

Monsignor Leopold, as he often did, dedicated the mass that May morning to the dead of the war and the dead of the Holocaust. He asked God to receive the souls of those lost, to welcome them into His kingdom, and to grant them eternal life in the world to come: the world with no beginning and no end, where all good and true souls would stand united for all time.

After the mass, Lisel stayed and prayed the Stations of the Cross. Slowly, with great devotion, she walked the circuit of St. Winfried's, kneeling before each image. In this way she followed Christ from Pilate's chamber, through the streets of Jerusalem, and to Golgotha. She travelled with him as he carried the burden of his cross, falling three times amid the mocking crowd. Then she bore witness as he was stripped and nailed to the cross, at last being laid in his tomb – the holy blood having been spilled, the cruel day having ended, the round stone having been rolled across the mouth of the cold cave.

Lisel held many secrets close inside her. Just one of them, and certainly the least, was that when Eli was a baby she'd quietly brought him to St. Winfried's and had him baptized. She'd not even told Jurgen. The infant cried when Monsignor Leopold poured holy water over his forehead. The baby frowned and stared up at her as if he knew she were engaged in some sort of intrigue. But she was glad, nonetheless. There was no harm, and it made her feel better.

She was sorry for all that had happened so many years before. But she'd known no better. She'd been raised with it. And she was so young. The Jews had killed Christ, after all. Her teachers taught her this, her and her sister. Condemned by Almighty God himself to their endless wandering diaspora, the Jews were no more German than they were any other race: mere vagabonds and parasites whom – it was rumored – offered blood sacrifices of Christian babies during dark rituals in secret places. The nuns said it themselves, albeit in whispers. Films in the cinema showed them as rats: filthy, multiplying, breeding disease and corruption. And wasn't it the Jews who had overthrown the old order in Russia, imposing atheism and Communism across half of two continents?

So she and her sister went with the others. They joined the mob. They dragged their friends and neighbors from their homes, sacked their properties, and handed them over for relocation. Then her sister met an SS guard assigned Chelmno, a man whose brother ranked high in the same jack-booted church, and married him.

It had not taken Lisel long to see things differently. That dark, starless winter night in their little town, that night of crying children and terrorized elderly men and women – that night proved a strange, perverse blessing which opened her eyes.

But she'd not been brave, had she? She'd not spoken out. She'd retreated and married and sent her young husband, a good man of the Wehrmacht, off to battles in which he died. Only afterwards did she speak, once all the battles were lost. Only in defeat did she raise her voice, become an outcast in her little town where so many remained loyal to the old order, and come here to Bonn – hoping the horrors were ended.

She'd been so grateful for her job back in those cruel early days after the war – not just for the small salary which allowed her to live, but for the goodness of the work itself, the opportunity to, in some small way, make amends. In her mission with the Red Cross she'd spent ten hours a day taking registrations from survivors, cross-referencing these with other registrations and camp records, at times helping loved ones find one another amid the post-war chaos, at other times (most often) delivering heart-breaking news gleaned from the Nazis' painstaking liquidation records. But this she viewed as her penance, her punishment, her exercise in bearing witness if not to the horror, then at least to its aftermath. This was her way of confronting, acknowledging, and admitting the past. She'd done that penance for more than twenty years, until retiring. But she still felt the guilt and pain.

*

Jurgen could not believe his eyes.

"Well you certainly seem surprised!" said Wilfried, flashing a grin at both Rubin and Kreigsman.

"*Surprised* is not the word. I don't even *know* a word for this."

"*Astonished*, perhaps?"

"That is closer for sure. Wilfried, what is this? Explain to me, please. What's going on?"

"That I will do," he replied, sitting down.

"My friends here are annoyingly cryptic, are they not? Too fond of riddles. Very maddening. They love the 'cloak-and-dagger' thing a bit too much. They perform as if they are in a movie. They delight in drama, as when they tossed that name *Enkert* at you, like a spear. Oh yes. I've been listening. I don't even know why Rubin bothered to summon me. I was about to be on my way. Another bit of play-acting!"

"Wilfried, about my identity ..."

"Yes. Please forgive me for sharing this information, this confidence, with my friends here. But believe me, it was very necessary."

Wilfried looked at Rubin.

"Rubin, give Jurgen a drink. He's earned it. Let's have some pity and settle his nerves!"

"Good idea. I should have thought of that earlier. Where are my manners?"

"Locked in your closet," said Kreigsman, "along with your good looks."

All three of the men chuckled. Wilfried seemed completely at home with the other two, as though they were old colleagues.

Rubin stood, turned to a small cabinet, poured some schnapps, and handed the glass across his desk to Jurgen.

"One also for me," said Kreigsman.

"Of course," Rubin sighed.

Once he had his drink in hand, Kreigsman turned to Wilfried.

"The floor is yours," he said.

Wilfried nodded.

"Jurgen, you will remember not too long ago we both noticed in the newspaper the death of one Johannes Frankl, a former Auschwitz guard, quite sadistic, whom inmates used to call 'the beast with the whip.'"

"Yes, he was found with his throat cut in a barn near Oberammergau, where he'd been living under an alias. The police received an anonymous note citing his crimes and saying he'd been executed by ... I forget what they called themselves."

"Those Who Will Not Forget."

"Yes, that's it. At first the police thought the note a hoax. But when they went to the barn they found

Frankl there, quite dead. He'd been prominent in the community, I believe. One of the lead organizers of the famous annual passion play."

Wilfried nodded and waved his arm in the direction of Rubin and Kreigsman.

"Well, you are now sitting with *Those Who Will Not Forget*. At least some of us."

Jurgen glanced at the two other men, who nodded in affirmation.

"It was Kreigsman's idea," Wilfried continued. "He convinced Rubin and I to embark on this adventure a few years ago. Of course, we are a bit old to go around slicing people's throats. There are others with more youth and stamina who generally do jobs like that, though Mr. Kreigsman here sometimes becomes personally involved whenever there's a case in which he has a special interest. Generally, however, we three are more concerned with ..."

"With what you might call *research*," Kreigsman chimed in.

"Yes. *Research. Investigation.* A more fitting occupation for old men."

"I'm amazed," Jurgen said.

"We've been at this for only a few years," said Wilfried. "My two compatriots here are both former concentration camp inmates. They've got the scars and the tattoos to prove it. They each narrowly escaped with their lives, but lost their wives and their children. I, on the other hand, was not so unfortunate. But then I was not a Jew. I was what some these days call a 'Righteous Gentile' in that my wife and I protected dear Ruth at some risk to ourselves. But that was all we did, and in retrospect it was not enough given the horror with which we were confronted."

"It was plenty," said Kreigsman. "Stop beating yourself up. I'm sick of hearing all your fucking *mea culpas*. Give it up."

Wilfried paused for a moment, then continued.

"We always hear about the romantic celebrity Nazi war criminals – Mengele and men with equally prominent histories, also the men who orchestrated genocide from on high: senior SS officers, magistrates, and so forth, many of them hiding in distant South American outposts, and many untouchable. Most of these especially notorious personages have the connections and money to make themselves secure in distant places. Sure, the Israelis got Eichmann, but he's pretty much the exception to the rule. And a big part of the reason Eichmann wound up being caught was, despite his former prominence in the Reich, he didn't have any money protecting him. He was no longer particularly relevant to them. Or perhaps even of more value to them as a sacrificial lamb."

"I can see that," said Jurgen.

"But we don't hear much about the *real* operatives, the *real* killers, do we? The men – *and women* – at the levers. We don't hear about the cobblers and accountants and school-teachers who, once they put on the Death's Head uniform, became mass-executioners: the workers at the wheel of 14 million murders – six million Jews, two million Poles, five million Russians, half a million Gypsies, and half a million non-Jewish Germans. Some of these thugs were caught; some were executed. But many still walk the streets alongside us. A good number – those who received slaps on the wrist and so-called *deNazification*, or a few years in prison – live openly under their real names. But the very worst of them, the most truly barbaric perpetrators, the most truly accomplished sadists and brutes, many with death sentences issued in abstentia, also live either here or elsewhere in Europe. They do so under new identities, protected by close networks of their brethren."

"This is not really news, Wilfried."

"Of course this is not news. But it is also unacceptable. Justice *must* be done. We sitting here have taken on the task. Those whom the courts have sentenced to die, must die, as must others who have evaded real justice."

"So? You want to kill my father once he returns? Go ahead. I really don't care."

"No," said Rubin from behind the desk. "We want to *use* your father. And we want you to help us use him."

"I don't understand."

"Of course not," said Wilfried. "Not yet. But you will before we are done."

"Alright then."

"I've mentioned the self-help networks of these criminals. Something like mutual-aid societies. Largely, though not entirely, secret."

"Yes."

"They frankly permeate our society. The official networks of the courts and police – most especially the police – are riddled with former Nazis who quietly and quite informally cooperate in protecting the men we seek. Fraudulent identity cards. Helping place people in jobs. Papers to bolster concocted histories which place men in the Wehrmacht on the

Russian front when in fact they were at Aschwitz-Bierkenau. That sort of thing."

"Of course. Stands to reason."

"There are only two more formal organizations of which we are aware. The first, and most public, is Silent Aid, the face of which is Helga Rath, the daughter of Erich Raff, one of Himmler's chief aids, who was hung at Landsberg in 1946."

"I think I've heard of it, and her."

"Yes. Well, Helga is something of a celebrity in Nazi and neo-Nazi circles. She's seen as a link to the upper eschelons of the past. There are photographs of her sitting on Hitler's lap when she was a young girl, and all of that sort of garbage. So all the old comrades want to shake her hand."

"I understand."

Wilfried nodded.

"Raff's Silent Aid very actively provides legal representation for former SS men who find themselves on trial. They as well deliver relief assistance to former SS men who've served sentences and returned to the street needing help. Additionally, we believe the organization cooperates with others in financing, shielding, and sheltering those on the run. Of course, the latter cannot be verified. By that I mean *proven*. But there is little doubt."

"Understood."

"Then we have the well-funded ODESSA which – though highly secretive in its operations – needs no introduction. I say well-funded because the organization is rich with gold and jewels and art smuggled out of Europe, or at least hidden away in Europe, by the SS near the end of the war, once they saw all was lost. In short, they pay for their operations with the wealth of those they murdered."

"Yes, yes," Jurgen said. "Everyone knows this story."

"The ODESSA," said Rubin, taking up the thread, "tends to be multinational, while Silent Aid tends to be strictly local. Nevertheless, the ODESSA also remains quite active in shielding SS murderers right here – not just in South America or other distant places. From what we've been able to learn, there is one man in particular who is the 'point-person' for European contact and operations. We don't know exactly where he is, though we do know he's in Germany and we know his name. By that I mean we know his *real* name, his true identity, although he most certainly lives and works under an alias."

"Yes?" said Jurgen.

"We are talking about you're uncle. Your father's elder brother. The man after whom you are named: SS-Gruppenführer Jurgen Enkert."

"Impossible! There's been no sight or word of him since the end of the war. He's become a myth. A ghost. He's more of an illusion than even Mengele. He's probably dead. And even if he's alive, he's so far off the map no-one will ever find him."

"You are wrong. He's quite alive and he's *in* Germany. We have this on good authority. What is more, he is central to the operations of the ODESSA throughout Europe."

"But isn't he, himself, under a death sentence?" said Jurgen. "He was one of the main administrators. An efficiency expert – and all too good at it, from what I've read."

"Yes. For that alone we'd love to find him," said Rubin. "But even more importantly, we feel that he, as the chief match-maker for fugitive SS men in need of help and those able to provide help, is bound to have records which will be invaluable in helping us find other criminals. All of these Nazis, especially these administrators, have always been so devoted to record-keeping. It is a fetish with them. We believe if we find the man we will find the paperwork."

"As for you," said Kreigsman, crushing out a cigarette – his fifth or sixth, Jurgen had lost count – "given your blood-relation, and the fact of your father's pending return, we see you as the ideal candidate to help us infiltrate and find your uncle. Your father's return will, hopefully, give you good reason. You know, the loyal old soldier will want to see his brother again, and who better to help make that happen than his own loyal son?"

"You're wrong," answered Jurgen. "I won't be of any use. I'm married to a Jew and have a son who is a Jew. I'm a *liberal*. I've been enrolled and active in more than one anti-fascist organization, both in college and after. I'm nothing like them, and one look at my history will show them I'm nothing like them."

"Don't you see?" answered Kreigsman. *"That's how we know we can trust you!"*

"Let me explain," said Wilfried. "It is Jurgen *Todt* who is married to a Jew and has done all the things you speak of. Your Tante Lisel has layed wonderful ground-work by effectively washing Jurgen Enkert the younger off the face of the earth. *There is no Jurgen Enkert of Bonn*, is there? No such person exists. In fact, there is no record of *you* as Jurgen Enkert *anywhere*. That's why we'll be free, with our contacts, to manufacture records for you, verifiable records. The ODESSA has its friends; we also have ours."

"And if I find him?" asked Jurgen. "What then? I'm no murderer you know. I won't kill him for you."

"No," Kreigsman answered. "Don't worry. We merely want a name and an address. Your uncle's alias and his location. That is all. We will take care of everything else, and you will go home to Bonn. You will return and go on with your life as Jurgen Todt, a buyer of old crap and a seller of precious antiques."

Jurgen raised his eyebrows.

"Nothing personal," said Kreigsman. "A joke! Why does everyone take my jokes personally?"

"Because you're an ass," Rubin answered.

Kreigsman shrugged.

"Maybe so."

Wilfried cleared his throat loudly.

"Now, as to the approach ..."

Wilfried outlined the plan and secured Jurgen's reluctant agreement. Rubin said details would be finalized in due course. They did not expect the return of Jurgen's father until August at the earliest. For the immediate future all further contacts would come through Wilfried.

After Jurgen left, the three elders sat together and continued their conversation.

"Well, gentlemen," said Wilfried, "let's hope we do not wind up ripping up *too much* of the past with this little adventure. Some things should remain in the ground. I may be a Catholic, but even I know not all resurrections are good. We must be careful."

*

And thus it began.

Chapter 3

The phone call had gone well. "I merely told her who I was," Jurgen explained to Kreigsman when they rendezvoused at the bar. "Then I requested to see her. Of course, my name got her attention immedaitely. She asked me to explain the connection, whch I did. When she inquired about what I needed, I explained briefly and asked if I might have an appointment to go into things further."

Just like the night before, they sat far away from all others, at the shadowed end of the bar, and conversed in low tones.

"So?" said Kreigsman.

"So, I go to a party she throws tonight. She says these are people I should meet."

"Excellent. Wonderful. You got through it fine."

"I was nervous. *I still am nervous.* But I will do alright I guess."

"You have struck gold," said Kreigsman. "This is excellent. Rath's social circle, you must understand, is rather limited. Think about it. Who in Germany today wants to associate with a known, unapologetic Nazi – not to mention one with so odious a name as *Rath*?

No one, of course, except other unapologetic Nazis. You will probably be in the thick of things tonight. Don't drink too much. Keep your wits about you."

"Wonderful," said Jurgen, without enthusiasm.

The thought of being surrounded by such people made him cringe.

"And you must know you will be something of a celebrity there, just like Rath. They will *love* you. I'm sure that is part of the reason why she has invited you. Here you are: another member of the next generation who wears what they think of as a great name, supposedly wears it quite proudly, and shares in their vision, values, and loyalties. *By God, you'll wind up signing autographs!*"

"Wonderful," Jurgen repeated, with even less enthusiasm.

"Very good! Let me know how it goes. I won't say to you to have a fun time, but please certainly go ahead and have an interesting time. *And be sure to shower afterwards.*"

"Very funny."

"So, what else did you do today? I hope you relaxed. That was an order you know!"

"I walked around. I saw some sights. I went and prayed in the cathedral. I visited a synagogue."

"Good Catholic boy visits synagogues!"

"Well, only after I went to a church. First things first!"

Kreigsman caught the eye of one of the bartenders and held up two fingers, signaling another round. Jurgen by now had realized Kreigsman really enjoyed his drinks, but he never appeared drunk and never seemed to skip a beat.

"Churches, synagogues," Kreigsman said, pondering. "I met a priest in the camp. A very brave priest. Name of Schiller. I remember his great long curly beard made him look like Rasputin. Evidently he and some other priests had been hiding Jews in their priory. They weren't very good at it. They fucked up. They got caught. Schiller wound up at Auschwitz, in the same barracks as Rubin and myself."

"Rubin was at Auschwitz?"

"Yes. You didn't know? That is where we met. A match made in Hell. Anyway, one night there was an escape from the barracks, a successful escape, after which – according to camp rules – ten men got randomly selected to be starved to death. Retaliation, you see. Right before the guards took the ten away, Schiller stepped forward and asked to be allowed to take the place of one of the condemned – a man with a family, whereas Schiller, being a priest, had none. It really surprised me when the SS captain agreed. I thought Schiller would just wind up getting added to the group, making it eleven, or be shot on the spot. You never knew. But that did not happen. It was a great act of courage on the part of Schiller. I respected him after that."

"Not before?"

"Well, yes and no. Sure, I mean, he'd been brave in harboring Jews. But in the camp, I don't know, he said things I thought stupid given the circumstances, and with which I still do not agree. Otherwise I would not be here."

"Things such as?"

Kreigsman shrugged and took a drag on his cigarette.

"My bunk was right above his, you see. In the night, in the dark, other Catholics would sneak over to him, make their confessions, and seek counsel. He was always telling them to forgive their tormentors, to forgive the murderers – all that *They Know Not What They Do* bullshit. Trust me, they knew."

Kreigsman paused as the next round arrived. He downed half his glass in one large gulp. Tonight he was drinking sherry, and had ordered the same for Jurgen.

"I remember one particular SS officer – an especially bestial thug who seemed to have a particular interest in tormenting Schiller. I forget the pig's name. He had a large birthmark on his cheek, a weird kind of bluish birthmark I've never seen the like of before or since. Anyway, one day for no apparent reason this sadist took Schiller, stripped him of his shirt, and bound his wrists to a massive, heavy oak plank: a crossbeam. Once this was done, he and some other SS men marched Schiller around the camp: parading him, mocking him, shoving him onward, kicking him whenever he fell, and beating him with a whip, as if herding an animal. So what happens? Later that night I hear Schiller praying for the SS officer by name, asking God to forgive him. *Insanity.*"

Jurgen had no answer.

"That SS demon with the face, he was a real psychopath. One of the worst. He especially liked to brutalize children. I saw him grab the newborn of a Russian woman, taking it with both hands by its head and throwing it into a pile of corpses. I saw him put another newborn baby into a burning barracks stove. He seemed to take special joy in inflicting misery on

Jewish holy days. He burned two hundred children alive on a massive open fire on the night of Yom Kippur, 1943. I saw it with my own eyes. I was made to help build the fire – although we were not told what it was for. Once the huge blaze was underway, a group of SS officers led by the circus freak arrived on motorcycles. They circled the flames several times, as if in some sort of pagan ritual, before pulling off to the side. A moment later came several trucks – dump trucks, ten of them – loaded with children. None of the children looked to be more than five or six years old. The trucks backed up to the flames, and just poured the children in. The screaming. I still hear the screaming. Some tried to crawl out, but were beaten back by SS guards carrying batons. I heard later they'd all come from a Jewish kindergarten. The man with the fright mask laughed and laughed. Cackled. Of all the horrors, that was the worst."

Kreigsman polished off his sherry with another large gulp, then signaled to the bartender for another. This time he raised only one finger, as Jurgen had not touched his latest drink. (He did not possess Kreigsman's capacity.)

"As for that priest: he was a good man," Kreigsman sighed. "Just *too* good."

"I suppose."

"But enough of all that!"

Kreigsman patted Jurgen on the back.

"You are doing excellent work. I tell you frankly, I was unsure at first. *An amateur I said, and an antiques dealer! He won't have the guts. He won't have the fire. He'll be like every other German. Lazy. Afraid. Wanting to leave the past buried. Wanting to pretend all is well, and there's no more can be done.* At first Rubin agreed with me, you know. But then we both respect Wilfried a great deal, and he expressed so much faith. So we became convinced."

"How did you two meet Wilfried?"

"*Oh, through channels*, let us say. The Nazis have their networks? Well, so do we 'good guys.' And it says something about history, I believe, that today all the Nazi networks involve hiding and running, while ours involve hunting and chasing. We're on top. *Us.* Yesterday's victims."

The bartender placed Kreigsman's drink before him.

"Here," he said, lifting his new glass. "We drink now. We drink to those gone, but also to the living, and to the mission taken up by we who are left behind. We drink to tidying up loose ends, sweeping up remnants, and stomping out whatever embers still burn from a fire already dead."

With less enthusiasm than he would have liked, Jurgen joined Kreigsman in the toast.

*

Her most ardent admirers sometimes called Helga Rath the pin-up girl of the Fourth Reich. She delighted in the description. At age forty-five she was still slim, with a perfect shape: the most tapered of waists, the longest of legs. Her sunrise-blonde hair flowed down to her shoulders and curled slightly, naturally, at the ends. Her lips existed in a perpetual and alluring pout. Her eyes shown sea-blue between long black lashes. She always dressed and made herself up in a manner which highlighted these features, showing them to their best advantage.

After all, she'd been raised to take pride in her appearance. Her beauty was not the result of lazy happenstance or dumb luck. No, it came from discipline. She ate right, exercised, and kept her focus always on perfection: just as her father had trained her.

She stood in her living room and inspected herself in the large mirror above the fireplace. Below the mirror, on the mantle, sat her most precious possessions: photographs of herself as a child. In one she beamed while sitting on her father's lap. In another she held the hand of the Führer. In a third she cavorted with Eva Braun on the patio of the Berghof at Berchtesgarden. Towering Watzman, with all its white-capped alpine grandeur, rose behind them.

She remembered the fine Rath family mountain retreat not far from the Berghof, in the same vast compound where Speer, Bormann, Göring, and other party leaders maintained homes. She remembered the clear, clean ponds and streams. She remembered the green, verdant mountainsides. She remembered birthday parties in the Kehlsteinhaus, which the idiot Americans to this day called the "Eagles Nest," even though the translation of *Kehlsteinhaus* was *House on the Kehlstein*: the name of the mountain on which it sat.

Helga sighed. So much beauty now in ruins, leveled, gone forever. Only the Kehlsteinhaus and a few other structures remained. She'd visited just once. Rather than take the tourist bus, she hiked up the trail. Once she reached the top, the place seemed to her a tomb. The Kehlsteinhaus had been converted into a restaurant and seasonal biergarten where anyone – *anyone* – could freely enter. The large marble fireplace – that grand gift from Mussolini – stood brutally defaced, having been horribly chipped-away by American soldiers wanting souveniers. A museum on the lower floors preserved graffiti left by the conquerors, including crude pornographic drawings of the Führer in various obscene poses. She would have been horrified, but she'd expected nothing better.

Moving lower down the mountain, she visited the ruins of the Berghof and some of the other homes, including her own. Of the Berghof nothing remained except a part of the rear foundation. The grand house had been left a mere burned out shell after Allied bombing in '45. Of the Rath family retreat, only a remnant of fireplace stood, along with a small bit of foundation, all of this overgrown with wisteria and poison ivy. Walking away, she swore to herself she would never again return. The shattered and broken place made her cry, even though she rarely cried.

Only a few homes remained, including (ironically) the beautiful chalet and separate architectural studio of the traitor Speer, who'd demonstrated his cowardice at Nuremberg – apologizing, taking "responsibility" as the popular phrase went, and escaping the noose by becoming a lap dog for the victors.

She'd hoped he'd show himself to be a true man upon his release in '66. She'd hoped he'd recant, reveal his apologetics to have been cynical fabrications contrived to get out alive. But no. He kept right on swimming with the tide, taking the easy course, prostrating himself before the powers that be, allowing them to own him, legitimizing them and delegimitizing all that had been the greatness of the Reich.

She was proud her father had gone the other way. She was proud he'd remained true to Hitler, to the Reich, and to Germany till the end, making no excuses. Yes, he died at the end of a rope in Landsberg, but he died a German patriot, and with the dignity of an SS officer. She understood there was film which showed him marching bravely and confidently to the gallows, shaking hands with a warder, walking without hesitation up the thirteen steps, and refusing a hood. She'd never seen it, but hoped to one day. It would not make her upset or sad. It would simply make her stand taller.

But that had been her choice all along, hadn't it? As his daughter she could have hidden away, cowered, cringed from the light, changed her name. She could have shed all dignity, expressed outrage at her father's actions, paid lip-service to the false God of democracy, and joined most of Germany in telling itself lies. Her mother was somewhat inclined this way, but not Helga. She refused.

Next month, once again, she would travel from Berlin to the annual gathering at Ulrichsberg, Austria, to honor the dead and salute the surviving members of the SS. She would join others in bowing her head before the wall near the entrance to the grounds – the wall inscribed with the SS slogan "Die Ehre Unserer Soldaten Heisst Treue" (*The Honor of Our Soldiers is Their Loyalty*). Then in line she'd walk up to the memorial, located in a chapel at the top of the mountain. There – under the enormous cross visible for miles around – she would salute the plaques commemorating not only German SS veterans but also those from Austria, Denmark, Norway, Croatia, Spain, and Belgium.

She was not alone. The brothers Horst, Klaus, and Dieter Eichmann stood strong, didn't they? And now there was the young man with the infamous name who'd telephoned only hours before. Another comrade of the current generation. Another keeper of the flame. She looked forward to meeting him.

*

It took Jurgen only five minutes to walk from his hotel to the beer hall, called *Kaiserkeller*. The beer hall occupied the basement of a small office building. An illuminated sign announced the place. One walked down several steps to a subterranean entrance. A hand-lettered piece of cardboard hung on the large wooden door: "Closed for Private Party."

Jurgen entered.

A pretty young blonde sat behind a table in the small foyer. To the left of her stood a coat-rack, and behind her – through an archway – Jurgen saw a large bar, many seats and chairs, and a horde of people: the party in progress.

The blonde smiled and nodded to him.

"And your name, please?"

"Enkert," he said. "Jurgen Enkert"

The young lady indicated no particular recognition of the name. She simply scanned the list which lay before her, marked one line with a check, and said: *"Danka shön!* Have a wonderful evening."

Jurgen nodded and stepped through the archway.

He scanned the room: dozens of men and women, all of them old enough to be his parents. Each man appeared well groomed – neatly though inexpensively dressed. Simple jackets and ties. All the women made a quietly neat but economical appearance: a great deal of polyester. The over-riding feel one got was of ordinary middle-class respectability. Nothing more, nothing less, and certainly nothing ostentatious.

Most of the men stood in groups. They talked, laughed, shook hands, and slapped each other on the back – steins of beer in their hands. Most of the women sat at tables, some with beer and others with wine. They talked casually and happily amongst themselves.

Eyes turned briefly as Jurgen entered. A pause of just a moment. Quick glances of appraisal and curiosity before people turned back to their conversations. Jurgen guessed not many new faces were seen at such gatherings as these.

He walked to the bar and was about to order when he felt a firm grip on his arm. Turning, he saw an unsmiling middle-aged man, largely built, with a shaved head.

"You are Enkert," he observed. A statement, not a question.

"Yes."

"I am Otto."

"Nice to meet you."

Otto did not answer. He waved to the barman, who came right over.

"A beer for my friend. The good stuff. The same for me."

I'm his friend? thought Jurgen.

He tried to make conversation.

"Who is everyone?" Jurgen asked, nodding at the assembled.

"Comrades," Otto answered without enthusiasm. "Colleagues from old days. Germans."

The barman placed down two beers.

"Drink!" said Otto. His tone made the word sound more like an order than an invitation.

Jurgen obeyed.

"I have someone who wants to meet you," Otto said flatly.

He turned and signaled to a heavy-set man sitting at a table nearby. The man was bald, with bulging round eyes and an equally round face; also a pencil thin moustache so gray one could hardly discern it against his white skin. He wore a light tan suit. Standing, he approached the bar with a pronounced limp.

"This is Albert Steiner," said Otto. His tone suddenly seemed reverential and admiring. Then, with

no further word, he abruptly took his beer and walked away.

"Hello young man," Albert said cheerily. "Our
friend Otto is not much fun, is he? Not much of a
charmer."

"Not really."

"No. He never was. I think maybe someone was
mean to him when he was just a puppy. And now his
bite is even worse than his growl, I'm afraid."

Albert stuck out his hand.

"I am pleased to meet you, young Enkert."

"And I you."

"I'm afraid I do not know your good father, evidently a very efficient and loyal man. I'm told he has
recently risen from the dead."

"Yes, thankfully."

"I do, however, recall your uncle very, very well.
I knew him. Did some work with him."

"Really?"

Albert continued to smile.

"You look something like him. Yes. Indeed. I see a
resemblance."

Jurgen nodded.

"So," said Albert, getting to the point. "You look
for him? Your uncle?"

"Yes."

"I wish you luck. Many people have looked. No-one has found. Who knows if he is alive or dead?"

"Many people have looked," Jurgen agreed, "but no-one whom he might wish to have find him. I hope it may be different with me. And even if he is dead, I and my father would like to know."

"I understand. Family is very important."

"Exactly."

Albert shook his head.

"So many of our fine families have been seperated. It is all too common with us. We're left with our best men scattered around the globe: the back streets of Damascus, the mountains of Patagonia, God knows where else. They can't risk contact. Good friends of mine, some of them, whom I've not seen or heard from for years. Maybe they have their wives, their children. That's good. But their mothers and fathers grow old here, die. No visits for decades. No communication of any kind. Also brothers, sisters. We are talking about separations as final and impenetrable as the grave. It is truly tragic."

"So, no idea about my uncle?"

"Like I said: Who knows? It is just like, for instance, Mengele. I don't have a clue. Nobody in this room has a clue. Dead? Alive? In Brazil? In Mongolia? At Disneyland? Forget it. Trust me, that piece of scum Wiesenthal will figure this out before we do. Listen, I wish you well. But don't get your hopes up. If he's alive, he's laying very, very low. It would be quite a coup, would it not, for the Jews to get a hold of him as they did Eichmann? He's at the top of many lists. So, living or dead – either way he is deep underground."

"I understand."

"Come, let me get a beer and then I'll introduce you around. People will enjoy meeting you."

Albert walked Jurgen from group to group. Jurgen noticed each man straighten up just a bit whenever Albert came near.

Everyone was more than polite to Jurgen. In fact, quite gregarious and complimentary. "You wear a fine name!" said one old soldier. "I'm glad to see you wear it proudly. Not like some of those others!"

"He has his uncle's eyes," said one lady to another, loud enough for Jurgen to hear. "Don't you think he has his uncle's eyes? So handsome!"

The men praised. The women cooed. For the first time in his life, Jurgen got a small taste of celebrity. Kreigsman had been right – although no-one asked for an autograph.

The glow of Jurgen's attraction dimmed just slightly when the true movie star, Helga Rath, finally appeared. Everyone went to greet her, forming a line.

"They like to kiss the ring," Albert whispered. "Or maybe it is the ass. And she likes to have it kissed. You see? Isn't that sweet. Everyone is happy."

From his wry tone it seemed Albert, though to all appearances a Nazi through and through, nevertheless found much of the evening's goings-on absurd. He may have been a true-believer, yet his belief appeared to be laced with a large dose of ironic and sardonic cynicism. He seemed quite above it all, or at least above the people by whom he stood surrounded.

"Do you mind my asking why you limp?"

"A wound from the war. Right here in Berlin, actually. Very near the end of everything."

"Fighting the invaders!"

"No," Albert laughed. "Running away from them! Hitler was dead already. For several hours, in fact. Only idiots were still fighting – idiots and old men and little boys. When it was over the Russians shot the idiots, sent the old men back to what was left of their homes, and cuffed the ears of the little boys before marching them back to what was left of their houses, where they raped the mothers on what was left of the beds."

"You made it out?"

"Yes, to the American lines. Wearing a Wehrmacht uniform I took off a corpse. One didn't want to be identified as SS, or especially an SS officer. That would have been very bad for me."

"Everyone here, I take it, was SS."

"*Was. Is.* Just words. But they are all officially *de-Nazified,* therefore free to roam about under their own names. So let's toast deNazification!"

Albert raised his stein and clanked it against Jurgen's. They both drank, finishing their beers.

"We need another round!" Albert announced decisively. "But we'll have to wait, won't we, because here comes our hostess."

Rath moved through the crowd directly toward them, exchanging hugs and cheek-kisses with admirers as she went along.

"Albert," she said once she was close enough. "What a pleasure. I'm so glad you could make it. We don't see you often enough."

"I know. It is terrible. I should make an effort to be more social. I shouldn't be such a recluse."

"You mean you shouldn't be such a snob!"

"Guilty, perhaps. Who can say? But when I heard young Mr. Enkert would be joining the party, I just couldn't stay away."

She turned to Jurgen.

"Agh yes! Jurgen! So good to meet you. Albert has been entertaining you?"

"Yes, making me feel quite comfortable and welcome."

"These are wonderful people," said Rath. "The best. *Real* Germans. To be with them is heartening. An *affirmation*. Some things endure, Jurgen. People like you and me, it is good for us to be with these folk, to see them, to talk and share with them, the standard bearers of the older generation. They remind us what it is we have to live up to."

Jurgen nodded.

"Oh Helga," said Albert. "Please stop it with all the speeches! We know why we're here."

"And why is that?"

"Free beer."

Rath laughed.

"I did not think you liked beer."

"So, tonight I make an exception. Trying to be agreeable, you see. *Democratic*."

"Albert thinks I talk too much!" she said to Jurgen. "Lots of people think I talk too much. But that's just the way I am. *Loud and proud.*"

"Too loud!" Albert said, half-kiddingly.

"Never mind," she replied, putting her arms around his neck and giving him a kiss on the lips. "I still love you, you old beast!"

Before the night was done Jurgen had been introduced to everyone in the room, and had heard more stories about the "old days" than he ever wanted to hear again. Albert seemed to make a point of staying by his side. Jurgen could not help but notice how the man took the helm of most conversations, heading them one direction or another as he saw fit – dominating as though this were his second nature, and frequently seeking Jurgen's opinion on whatever topic happened to be hovering in the ether.

Only once did Jurgen see any sign of disrespect for Albert. Midway through the evening a quite non-descript man in a jacket and tie – gray hair, large belly, just like all the rest – walked over and drunkenly interrupted Albert in the middle of a story.

"What are you doing here?" he demanded. "*We* are the real men. The real workers. There are no officers here, because there are no longer any officers anywhere. All these here think we have to take your orders – but we don't. Your day is gone, your ..."

The man got no further before his wife rushed up, grabbed him by the arm, and began to pull him away. "Please forgive him, Obergruppenführer. He doesn't know what he's saying. He's always like this when he has too much beer. Always ..."

"Not at all," said Albert. "I understand completely. The drink can turn any one of us into a fool. Think no more about it."

"I'm no fool! I speak truth, you ..."

"Stop!" shouted his wife, "before you make real trouble. Come along! We leave now!"

A silence fell over the room as they exited, and lasted for more than a minute. Then, slowly, conversation returned.

"That is Martin, is it not?" Albert inquired, turning to the old soldier to his left. "The baker?"

"Yes, Obergruppenführer. He always takes too much beer and then always wants a fight, or just keeps talking stupid. You never know what he will say or do when he is in his cups."

"A sad habit," said Albert. "A very sad habit, I'm afraid. And sometimes a dangerous one. What is his last name again?"

"Metzler, sir."

"Oh yes. Metzler. Martin Metzler."

Later in the evening, when Jurgen found himself seated at a table with Albert and no-one else nearby, he asked what the older man did for a living.

"Oh," he answered, "I'm very boring. I'm lucky to have a small independent income. So, I don't do a damn thing. I kibbitz. I complain. I act the curmudgeon. I look at the sky. I talk incessantly to smart young men and bore them to tears. But let me tell you something ..."

"Yes?"

Albert suddenly grew serious.

"I suggest that you stay by the phone at your hotel tomorrow morning. You'll receive a call around ten, from somebody who can maybe help you."

"*Danka shön!*"

"Mind: I said *maybe* help you."

"Understood. Gratefuly understood."

At the conclusion of the evening the man who had first greeted Jurgen, the man named Otto – thoroughly intoxicated and boisterous – climbed atop one of the tables and led the entire group in singing the *Horst Wessel Song,* anthem of the Nazi Party.

Receive our salute; you died an honorable death!
Horst Wessel fell, but thousands newly arise
The anthem roars ahead of the brown army
The storm-divisions are ready to follow his path.

The flags are lowered before the dead who still live
The storm-division swears, his hand clenched into a fist,
That the day will come for revenge, no forgiveness,
When **Heil** *and* **Sieg** *will ring through the fatherland.*

As Otto sang, Albert leaned over and whispered into Jurgen's ear.

"Such a terrible song," he said. "Hideous. Almost as bad as the 'Star Spangled Banner.' But some people like it. God only knows why."

*

Kolm lay naked in bed with the equally-naked Ingrid asleep by his side. She'd done her job with precision. Drained him. With his little reading-light illuminating the pages, he indulged himself with one of John LeCarre's carefully crafted novels: a further adventure of that shrewd, astute, but essentially tragic British spook named George Smiley.

It was well after midnight by the time his bedside phone finally rang with the call he'd been expecting.

Kolm picked up: "Hello my old friend. So tell me your impression."

He listened intently for a minute or so.

"Very good. You think him genuine. I rely on your judgment. Thank you for this, Albert. You understand, there is no one else I could ask. ... Yes, good night."

Chapter 4

"Alright," said Kreigsman, sounding quite weary over the phone, "tell me about what a wonderful evening you had last night. Fill me in on all the charmers you met."

Jurgen wondered if perhaps Kreigsman was hungover. It certainly sounded as though he might be. No surprise there.

"The party was actually more boring than anything else," he said. "They were just a bunch of average, ordinary citizens for the most part. More nostalgic than dangerous. A bunch of old farts, in fact."

"You mean like me?"

"I didn't say that."

"Of course not. I'm just kidding. So, anyway, give me some names. It is always handy to have these facts in hand. You know, for the files. Who was where, and with who. Sometimes these details can be valuable."

Jurgen rattled off what names he could remember.

"Wait, wait. Hold on," said Kreigsman, evidently writing. "OK. Go ahead."

Once Jurgen was done with his list, Kreigsman said: "I recognize a lot of these bastards. The standard suspects. Mostly cowards and morons. The type who hold the torch and let it burn bright in private, but lay low otherwise."

"I got that."

"You made a good observation when you said they are, overall, more nostalgic than dangerous. These are generally nobodies whose greatest moment in life was when they served on the lowest rung of the supposedly elite SS. Now they are back to slinging hash or butchering cows or moving boxes from one side of a room to another. All they are good for, really. But it is still handy for them to have Jewish bankers to blame. The serious comrades, the ones who still go about real business – well, those guys don't pay much attention to them, in fact disrespect them, and would never trust any one of them with anything important. They were the janitors of the SS. Now they are the janitors of post-war Germany, nothing more. Of the people you mention, I'd only note two exceptions to this generalization."

"Yes?"

"Well, first of all, your Albert Steiner."

"Go on."

"He is no Steiner. The man you describe is clearly SS-Obergruppenführer Albert Pechstein. He is a fugitive. An international court convicted him in abstentia many years ago. We've no idea where he lurks. That he would brazenly appear at a Berlin party, let alone a party of known former SS members is, well, incredible – and I'm sure quite rare. I am truly amazed."

"Many people seemed surprised to see him, if that is a help."

"I don't doubt it."

"So," said Jurgen, "don't keep me waiting. Give me details about my new pal."

"Pechstein was one of the most prominent SS officers short of the very top tier. He personally oversaw the deaths of tens of thousands during assignments at a number of different camps. Near the end of the war, he received a promotion to become a junior adviser to Hitler himself. He was present in Hitler's Berlin bunker until the very day of Hitler's suicide. Then he somewhat miraculously escaped the city. Serge and Beate Klarsfeld – Nazi hunters equal to Wiesenthal, in my opinion – have done good research tracing his travels immediately after the fall of the Reich."

"Yes?"

"Although the Klarsfelds are not sure by what means, Pechstein made it to Rome not long after the fall of Berlin. There, he received aid from Bishop Alois Hudal, then head of Rome's Austrian-German Catholic congregation *Santa Maria dell'Anima*. Hudal was a true and devoted Nazi. He'd even written a book in the late 1930s full of praise for National Socialism and Hitler. After the war, Hudal organized so-called 'ratlines' by which many important Nazis escaped Europe. The list of people Hudal aided adds up to quite a creepshow: Stangl (the commandant of Treblinka), Eduard Roschmann (the Butcher of Rigga), Gustav Wagner (commander of Sobidor), even Eichmann and Mengele."

"How did Hudal help Pechstein?"

"Got him to Argentina on an Austrian passport with a fake name."

"And then?"

"Pechstein stayed in Argentina for fifteen years. So far as we know, he generally avoided the German community and didn't associate with other Nazis at all. Kept to himself. Maintained a low profile. He has family money, which his cousins somehow got to him on a regular basis, so he didn't have to work. He became something of an apparition."

"And why is he back?"

"He returned to Europe in 1960, right after the Mossad grabbed Eichmann. I guess he got nervous. We know he's been on the Continent ever since, but not where. Rather like your uncle, another ghost. The Klarsfelds and Wiesenthal say they doubt he is up to much, I mean with regard to today's circuit of active comrades. But now I think they may be wrong about that."

"Perhaps."

"I'll tell you what else I think."

"What?"

"I think the only reason someone like Pechstein would risk showing up at that gathering of dopes would be to check you out. Someone – and it would have to be someone with enormous clout, since Pechstein is nobody's errand boy – asked him to be there last night and to look you over. I'm sure of it. We are talking about a person with great authority – a person who would trust only the judgment of a comrade with Pechstein's prestige and experience. So, you see, this becomes quite intriguing."

"Yes?"

"Well, it appears a person unknown, a person of significant importance and power, thinks you very interesting. This is a good sign."

"Why is that?"

"It means you are not arbitarily going to be sent away, assuming you passed 'muster' with Pechstein last night. It means you are being taken seriously."

"Well, I suppose that's progress. But you said there was someone else of interest?"

"Yes, Otto Klemperer – though he never rose above the rank of *Unterscharführer* – is a most serious operational comrade. Officially deNazified, he is quite the thug nevertheless. The man is suspected in the postwar murders of several sadly-amateur Nazi hunters – murders which the police have pointedly *not* been strenuous in solving."

"A scary fellow."

"Yes. But this does not matter in regards to what we are engaged in right now. By the way, someone from Germany has already been at work inspecting your bonafides. Calls have been made to London University, the National Gallery, all the other places we expected. Jurgen Enkert, the graduate of London Univeristy with a degree in art and architecture, who lives in London's East End and restores paintings at the National Gallery – that Jurgen Enkert is well-installed and verified."

After a pause, Jurgen heard Kreigsman yawn. Loudly.

"Tired?" he asked.

"Well yes, but also a bit hungover to tell you the truth. I threw my own little party last night. A private party. No Nazis I'm afraid, but plenty of, well, just about everything else. I don't quite remember."

"You can't beat up on yourself like that."

"Really? I thought I just had."

"I mean ..."

"You know, I think you've been spending too much time with Saint Wilfried."

"It's just not good for you."

"Oh my? And I thought it was. Thank you so much for filling me in. Thank you for telling me what I already know."

"You're a smart man. Do you actually enjoy doing this type of thing to yourself?"

"In the night, I enjoy it just fine. In the morning, not so much."

"You shouldn't ..."

"Look, I have only four hobbies: chasing Nazis, sailing a bit on the Danube, drinking, and when I'm very lucky fucking a stray woman or two. I don't watch sports. They bore me. I don't gamble. I'm no good at it. I don't go to the damned opera. I'd rather stick needles in my eyes. And I don't write poetry, mostly because I hate poetry. I don't have my boat with me, and I can't find anyone to fuck. Thus I'm reduced to either making murderous criminals die or getting ossified. So leave me alone."

"Alright. Alright."

There was a silent pause at the other end of the line, then Kreigsman spoke again, this time far more somberly.

"Tell me something," he said. "Have you ever lived in a village all your life, from the cradle, been raised there just as your parents and grandparents before you, gotten married there, and begun to raise your children there, only to have your former good friends and neighbors one day stop talking to you, stop patronizing your family's business, stop allowing their children to play with yours, and even stop allowing your children to attend school?"

"No."

"Have you ever been forced to hide yourself and your family away in the basement of a barn owned by a kindly Christian, never going out in the light of day, living in constant fear of discovery by Gestapo or SS who will take you away and do God knows what with you?"

"No."

"Have you ever heard boots pounding the boards above your head in the middle of the night, been pulled from your blankets along with your wife and small children and your parents, then hauled up the stairs and out into a barnyard where you looked-on as laughing storm-troopers executed your friends, the man and woman who gave you shelter, leaving them in the snow to rot, the blood flowing out of them and making the snow beneath them turn red? Have you ever seen the blood of righteous people flowing out of them like rivers?"

"No."

"Have you ever been marched with your shivering wife and small children and parents through the winter night, thrown in the back of a truck, and taken to a trainyard where you were herded on a freight car with a hundred other terrified Jews, your children like all the others crying in shock and terror?"

"No."

"Have you ever stood on line at Auschwitz and had your wife, small children, and parents summarily sent off in one direction – which you learned only later, though not much later, meant immediate death – while you were sent off in another? Have you ever had that moment when absolutely everyone you loved was taken away from you, never to be seen again? To be transformed into ashes and cinder floating up the chimney of a crematorium?"

"No."

"Then with all respect, do not try to tell me how to live, or what is healthy and what is not. All that horror, all those blasphemous nights and days, all of it changed me. Now the only one thing I am truly good for is rendering justice. Nothing else. When not thus engaged, all I can do is try to forget as best I can, by any means possible. Maybe sometimes sailing. Maybe sometimes fucking. The rest of the time, *most of the time*, drinking. I hope you can understand that. But if you can't then just shut up anyway."

"I'm sorry."

"Don't be. It was not you. But leave me to what is left of my life."

"You are a good man."

"Really? You think so?"

"Absolutely."

"You know there is an old Yiddish saying. 'A righteous man who knows he is righteous is not righteous.' Self-conceit, you see. So, if only for that reason, I say I am not so sure. But we are what we are and we do what we do. God will know our face. He will understand or not. And that, my friend, is the extent of any wisdom I might have. Admittedly not much. Listen, we are done here. Give me a call after you hear from whatever son-of-a-bitch next reaches out to you, and we'll take it from there."

It did not take long. He spoke to Kreigsman again just a few hours later.

"A woman phoned around 10. I don't know who it was but she didn't sound like Rath. She told me to get to Bayreuth today, to check in to the Atlantia, and wait there for a call to set up a meeting. I don't know with who. Anyway, I'll leave shortly."

"Damn," said Kreigsman. "I was hoping they'd keep it local, the fuckers."

"Sorry."

"Alright. I'll leave soon as well, despite my pounding head. You'll be able to find me at the Bismarck. Still under the name *Gerber*. Got that?"

"Got it."

*

Ruth Todt sat beside her assistant and co-producer Dieter Ohlendorf in a small darkened room near the rear of the family apartment. As planned, Tante Lisel had taken Eli to her place for the day because Ruth did not want the child underfoot when she tended to such things as she did now.

A 35-millimeter projector cast its images over her shoulder onto a wall. The film – a rough cut of only one of the many interviews which would go to make her project – showed young blonde Dieter facing an older but clearly healthy and strenuous man: a striking figure with a set jaw, the shortest of short crewcuts, and sparkling white teeth. The man spoke confidently, happily, and proudly – convinced he was conversing with a young enthusiast, a fledgling comrade interested in documenting the history – *the real history* – of the Reich for those who would come after.

> *Dieter:* So please continue what you were saying.

SS-Unterscharführer Klaus Bauer: To answer your question – of course, I am still a Nazi. Nazism is the lens through which I – along with anyone else who is honest – looks at the world. You know: Our *weltanschauung*, yes? And in my heart I still wear the Death's Head.

Dieter: Explain what you meant when you said earlier the Jews caused their own problem.

Bauer: Well, I mean, all that "chosen people" stuff. They were better than everyone else, right? And they were bent on amassing all the wealth and power they could. They wanted to rule the world. At least the Western World. And look where we are today. Look at the 1,000 most powerful and wealthy families. Most are Jews. I tell you, the ones who were in Germany after the Great War caused a real catastrophe. They built great fortunes and became money-lenders while most Germans starved. After he came to power, Hitler tried to get rid of them. Think of the ones aboard that ship the *St. Louis*. No-one wanted them. Even America sent them back. So, then it was up to us to deal with the problem. Right?

Dieter: Of course.

Bauer: But even so, it was not so bad for them as is always told. The so-called "Holocaust" has been Hollywoodised by the Jews who run California. Anne Frank! Did she ever even really exist? Tell me that! Six million dead? How is this even possible? Show me the proof! Exaggerations abound. Did things happen? Sure. We are talking about war, after all. Desperate measures.

Dieter: You mean, whatever was done *had* to be done.

Bauer: Exactly. I say this emphatically. And I make no apologies.

Dieter: Of course there were deaths, but necessary deaths, am I right?

Bauer: Look, it is just simple logistics. Some swine bureaucrat in an office in Berlin keeps scheduling hundreds of train cars full of starving kikes to arrive at your camp every God damned day of the year. There's only so much space in the camp, and you've already got thousands more than it was designed to hold. There's no hygiene. There's not enough food. The whole place smells like one huge stinking latrine. So what do you do? Where do you put them? Look, they are as good as dead anyway.

Dieter: So one had little choice.

Bauer: There you have it. The only thing you can do is accelerate the inevitable. Minimize the suffering. Be efficient about it. We standing there, we SS who had been given our orders – we

didn't build the camp, we didn't schedule the trains. We just did as instructed
and solved the problem. That's all we
could do. No one particularly liked it.
We are talking about nasty work here.
But you couldn't let that bother you or
you would go insane. It is not as if we
could change anything, so we just carried on. And soon it became routine.

Dieter: The same with the harvesting?

Bauer: Well, the harvesting seems at
first glance to have been quite intoler-
ably mercenary. Right? The Elie Wiesels
of the world, in their paid speeches and
bestselling books, make so much of this
sort of thing. Great drama. But what we
are really talking about is pure econ-
omy. This is time of war. There are great
shortages all around. Nothing useful can
be wasted. *Nothing.* We don't have that
luxury, you see. So, yes, hair and all the

rest. I freely admit this. Tell me, do the dead need hair? Or gold teeth?

Dieter: Do you think you deserved to be jailed afterwards. Did you deserve what happened to you?

Bauer, shrugging: No. But it could have been worse. You know, it is ironic, and it shows how hypocritical people can be. I was an SS-Unterscharführer, a totenlager at the gas chambers. The lowest rank. In the first line, right? *Hands on.* But when these authorities who posture as great humanists finally brought me to court – in 1964 – and found me guilty, they sentenced me to just twelve years, and let me out after six. I read yesterday of a money launderer sentenced to twenty years without parole. So much for West German outrage over us so-called "murderers." Money crimes are more important to them than anything *we* ever did. Watch what the judges and prosecutors *do* rather than what they say.

Dieter: Do you think there is any sympathy today for the what the Reich achieved, or at least tried to achieve?

Bauer: Of course! How could that not be the case? Consider all the things Hitler warned about, so many of them coming true. But one has to be careful. It is still forbidden to speak of such matters in the way we're talking here. *And they say Hitler restricted free speech!* But since my release I've encountered many old comrades, and young people like you, and we've been able to talk truth to one another. This work you are doing, this film, is important. In another couple of decades there will be none who truly remember. All that will be left over is the Jew propaganda unless something is done. And you are doing it! I applaud you.

Dieter: Do you have anything you would like to add?

Bauer: Only this. Those of us who are lucky enough now to be truly free, and not hunted, we owe it to the rest to be proud. Each man must stand up. I was in a store not long ago and a man, I suppose a Jew, came up to me and jabbed a finger in my face. "I know you!" he said. "I remember you from Auschwitz! Murderer! Someone call the police! This is a war criminal!" Do you know what I said? I said "Fuck you! You're right, I was there. And I've done my time and it is over. Get away from me or it will be me who calls the police!"

Dieter: What happened?

Bauer: Nothing. Nothing at all! The wind went right out of that yidd's sails. It was a good day. He turned and walked away. He saw I was not afraid. More important, he saw I was not ashamed.

These Jews always think they have the upper hand, and then they are stunned to learn they do not!

The image went white. Just a ghostly square floating on the wall. The concluding strip of film slapped loudly, beating its rhythm from the projector's spinning top reel. Dieter stood, flipped the wall-switch for the overhead light, and turned off the projector.

"Yes, Dieter," said Ruth. "We are certainly *doing it.*"

"You know," said Dieter, "this one actually *knew* my father and worked with him. That's how I got to the man. He showed me old photographs of them together. He is so full of nostalgia this man. But that's good. His nostalgia clouds his caution and his judgment. He embraced me rather quickly, accepted me. There's a loneliness, isolation, and real need for vindication in a lot of these guys: a hunger for acceptance, also the reinforcement and enabling of their denial. And this one has already offered to introduce me around to others, not that I haven't been able to make the circuit pretty well already. It seems my parentage comes in useful for this project – the first time it has ever come in useful for anything."

Ruth pondered the similarities between Dieter and Jurgen. She wished she could confide things to Dieter. Not even Dieter knew Jurgen's real identity; they'd always kept this secret close. Still, perhaps someday there would be a good way for Jurgen to finally reveal himself – not just to Dieter, but to others as well. She hoped this would be the case, at least for Eli's sake. Otherwise Jurgen's family history would always be a dark lurking presence – one that could come out of the shadows on its own at any time, doing God-only-knew what kind of damage.

*

The bakery stood on Pfalzburger Straßen not far from Saint Ludwig's – in fact so close to the large Berlin church that the enormous steeple reflected in the glass at the front of the establishment.

The store comprised part of the ground floor of a small office building. Fresh-baked cakes, breads, and other offerings filled the window. Their tempting scents rushed out onto the street through the bakery's open door.

It was only 11. Otto had decided not to come too early – in part because of his own hangover; in part because he knew Metzler would not be likely to rise early either. Not after last night.

Otto stopped and looked on as a funeral procession moved slowly down the street in the direction of St. Ludwig's. First came a large black hearse, this followed by an equally large Mercedes limousine, also black with tinted windows. A mountain of flowers sat atop the wooden coffin in the back of the hearse. A dozen or so cars took up the rear of the procession, all bearing little purple flags to identify them as part of the contingent, and all with headlights switched on. They cruised at a dignified 20 miles per hour. The steeple bells began to toll just as the procession turned into the church driveway.

The scene seemed properly somber, although no one else on the street appeared to notice. Not the barber sweeping up in front of his shop. Not the grim fellow busy moving boxes of iced fish out of a van and into a seafood store. Not the brawny young man busily tightening the screws on the engine of his motorcycle. Not the girls who walked by him: ogling, giggling, and whispering amongst themselves. And not the weary Martin Metzler, whom Otto now spotted wandering quite lethargically and slowly down the sidewalk towards his place of business.

As Metzler came close, Otto smiled and reached out to him.

"Hello, my friend. I need some of your good bread!"

"And you shall have it!" Metzler answered, perking up at the sight of his comrade.

Otto reached around with his left arm to embrace Metzler, and with his right hand jabbed a long, sharp knife into the baker's lower stomach. Once it was well in, Otto quickly stood back as the dark blood began to flow. Metzler stared at him with wide-eyed amazement before collapsing down to his knees, then falling over onto the sidewalk.

As Metzler gasped for breath, Otto turned and walked toward the busy intersection just a block to the north. He was just about to turn onto the boulevard when he finally heard a scream of discovery. He did not look back. He turned the corner and soon merged into the safe anonymity of the city.

*

The drive was not unpleasant. With Ruth in the car it would have taken him four hours or more to cover the 355 kilometers. Without her telling him to slow down it took just a little over three, even with a short break for food once he was well into the West. After he ate, he used a call-box to get in touch with Ruth.

"I'm on my way to Bayreuth," he told her. "Hopefully my last stop before heading home."

"You must be tired."

"Yes, and lonely."

"Mmmm. Me too ..."

"I think we'll be making some noise when I get back."

"Good thing Eli sleeps so soundly!"

"Yes indeed," said Jurgen. "So, what is going on? Anything new?"

"No. Wilfried called to see how we are doing. Dieter and I are working hard on the editing. But he still has a number of interviews to shoot. Oh, and we went to a wonderful concert at the synagogue. It was Mahler. *Quartet for Piano and Strings*. We all enjoyed it."

"Sounds superb." (Secretly, he reveled in the fact that he was so far, far away. He much preferred Mick Jagger.)

"So," she said. "I gather you have another contact to make."

"Yes."

"With who?"

"Damned if I know."

"But you are safe?"

"Yes, I'm sure. So far everyone loves me. In fact it seems quite strange how well I fit in."

"Well, soon it will be over, hopefully."

"And now I'd better get back on the road."

"Good. Alright. Call me again soon. I love you."

The remainder of the drive took him through a lush valley of rich farmland: a steady flow of hop, barley, and wheat fields punctuated by quaint farmhouses and massive barns. All was plentiful, idyllic, bucolic. The countryside throbbed with the pulse and peace of simple living.

Still, he couldn't help but wonder whether one of these picturesque barns had been the one under which Kreigsman and his family cowered. He imagined what scenes likely played out across this verdant landscape during the Nazi era, and what black tales the good ground could tell were it to speak. He wondered what ghosts roamed the fields at night, and the things the dead might know that we could not.

If you just looked, and didn't think too much, this and so much of the rest of rural Germany seemed a simple, beautiful, naïve place of storybook villages, wide fields, and ancient churches: picture postcard snaps suitable for ads in travel magazines – slices of sublime agrarian romanticism just like those encouraged in art during the reign of Hitler.

Paintings like this were not hard to come by – works which mythologized and attempted to eke great mystic truths from otherwise rudimentary and facile images. Pictures which strove to merge race with place, and suggest a spiritual unity between blood and soil. Such canvases had been churned out by the hundreds throughout the 30's and early 40's. These days, at any auction you attended, you could count on finding a dozen or more stacked upon a table at the end of the evening, unsold.

It was astonishing, he thought, the amount of true and utter naïvete which had come bundled with the dark reality of the Nazis. Not only works of visual art, but also films and other media routinely portrayed a fantasy-land of noble Teutonic youth striving happily for physical and mental excellence, joyous families thriving in a racially and culturally perfect civilization, and spiritual and ethnic comradeship transacted on a scale too absurd to think real. From a distance, you really had to admire how the triumphal panacea shown in Nazi propaganda so efficiently obliterated reality. Such masterful sleight of hand.

The Nazis displayed special prowess in wielding ancient symbols and myths, bending them to their purposes. What poetry: the spiritual inevitability of triumphant racial supremacy paired with the idea of a great pagan trinity encompassed in the cosmic vision of the Führer/Savior: Father, Son, Holy Ghost. As a Father, the Führer acted as the reawakened Barbarosa here to fulfill destiny, here to lead the Aryan people on a divine mission of race and conquest. At the same time, the Führer served as the son of Providence: the mystical source of that life-spirit (Holy Ghost) which was the volk. How trite and ridiculous. A modern, ruthless fascist state based on fairytales.

No wonder Hitler loved Richard Wagner so much, Jurgen thought as he approached the heart of Bayreuth from the north and drove past Wagner's grand Festspielhaus. Like the heroes of Wagner's *Der Ring des Nibelungen* cycle of operas, Hitler had sought the magic ring which would give him incarnate power to rule the world: absolute dominion. But also like those heroes, in the end Hitler's quest for the ring did nothing but cause him to destroy himself, and his people.

After passing the festival grounds, it took Jurgen just a few minutes to get to his hotel.

Unlike Berlin's King Frederick, the Atlantia was a starkly modern structure of glass and steel, complete with transparent elevators and a covered rooftop swimming pool. One could not miss the large and ridiculous fountain which dominated the lobby. A macabre marble statue of the brave but doomed Wagnerian hero Siegfried stood in the middle, an eternal stream of water inexplicably issuing from his mouth. *Better that than his prick*, Jurgen thought.

As the voice on the phone had told Jurgen to expect, the desk held a reservation in his name. He wound up with a small suite on the fifteenth floor, one overlooking the hotel front and the city center. Still tired from his strenuous night, he took a long slow shower and then ordered room service: sauerbraten, and a good beer. Once he finished eating, he lay down for a nap. It was 3 pm.

The phone woke him two hours later. The same female voice.

"Mr. Enkert?"

"Yes."

"I trust your journey was a good one."

"Yes, quite nice. Beautiful country and a beautiful day."

"And your suite? Suitable?"

"More than suitable, thank you."

"It is the best place in town. Lots of the other Bayreuth hotels, despite their age and aesthetic appeal, are nothing but dust-traps with plumbing as old as their ornamentation."

"Well, I appreciate you steering me straight."

"Now, to business."

"Yes."

"I've been instructed to warn you that there is no guarantee. In fact it is quite doubtful the gentleman with whom you'll meet will be able to help you with your search."

"I understand."

"There is, however, a complete willingness to put some feelers and inquiries out to see if we can't at least help you with some leads or, depending on circumstances, verify the death of your uncle. At this moment, to tell you the truth, no-one we know can say for sure whether he's alive or dead. Anyway, we will do all we can."

"I appreciate that."

"Prior to meeting, I've been instructed to ask you what *you* can tell *us* about your uncle as regards any family lore of his story after the end of the war."

"There is really nothing. He was never spoken of. I know only what my father told me the other day."

"And that is?"

"He was informed by comrades at the time that his brother had somehow made it out of Germany through the American lines and then to Austria, where he joined a small group of SS refugees who were planning to hike over the mountains into Italy. Whether any of this is true or not, I have no idea. Anything could have happened. He could have died trying to get away from the Soviets and been tossed into a ditch. He could have been killed by the Americans and tossed into a ditch. He could have died on the trek over the mountains. He could be running a ski lodge in northern Italy. He could be in a grave in Argentina. In short, my father is the only one who knows anything, and what he knows might very well be nothing. The whole thing is, as the saying goes, 'a riddle wrapped in an enigma.'"

"That narrows it down!," she joked. "He's either nowhere or anywhere."

"Well, not quite anywhere," said Jurgen, continuing in the same vein. "We can pretty well cross Jersualem off the list."

"Yes, I'll do that right now! You're funny!"

"As soon as I get this uncle thing sorted out, I'm going to Las Vegas to make my fortune as a comedian."

"You should."

Jurgen marveled he was actually able to make light-hearted jokes regarding any of this, but supposed it just meant he was getting into his character – which was probably the safest place to be.

"So," said the woman, "do you have a jacket or sweater with you?"

"Yes. Both."

"Let's see. It shouldn't be too cool tomorrow morning. What color is your sweater?"

"Red."

"Alright. Tomorrow I want you to wear your sweater, or if you are too warm just drape it over your shoulders. It will help us find you when we meet."

"Yes, so when and where?"

"I'm getting to that. Write this down."

Jurgen took the little courtesy pad and cheap, logo-emblazoned courtesy pen from the bedside table and wrote down the voice's directions for what he was to do and where he was to go the following morning. Later on, after visiting the hotel lounge for a few more beers, he returned to his room, telephoned "Mr. Gerber" at the Bismarck with all the latest news, and collapsed into bed.

Chapter 5

That night Jurgen had a profound dream which felt like memory. Vivid. Laced with the immediacy of suddenly resurrected truth. Images and sounds long forgotten. Infinitely more real than nostalgia.

A picnic. A delightful holiday. In the distance one could see the vast manor house – which he remembered being called variously the *castle* or the *schloss*. Quite near it stood the beautiful white church with its large steeple scraping the sky. The wide river wound behind both buildings.

A summer day. Warm, delightful, with a fresh breeze coming off the water. Somber men in dirty pajama-like clothes carried food-trays from the castle and placed them on tables. Equally somber men in uniforms, holding machine guns, stood at a comfortable distance, watching.

Jurgen's father and uncle, as well as several others, kicked balls back and forth with Jurgen and the other boys. Laughter. Shouts. Pretty little girls in freshly washed cotton dresses played on the swings and the slide. The men wore civilian clothes but issued orders to those carrying trays; sometimes even to those who stood guard.

The landscape seemed a fairyland, at least to the eyes of a child: the high white steeple, the large and beautiful castle, the tranquil river, and the playing field and playground full of delights.

His mother sat with the other ladies – some at tables, some in lawn chairs. Men in pajamas held parasols over the ladies' heads. The ladies chatted banal niceties which he could neither have heard nor understood as a child, but perceived – albeit distantly – in his dream. The weather. The fashions. The German Women's Club in town: the only social life, since so few of the people here spoke German. The swimming in the river. How refreshing, so long as one went at the right time of day.

Smoke rose in the distance – a large fire of some kind, beyond the trees but (somehow he knew) not *of* the trees. In his dream, he understood the fire to be a regular daily rite, a ritual, an anticipated rising of smoke and ash as punctual as the noonday bell.

Later on, also in the distance: another daily ritual. A hundred or so men, women, and children walked slowly from the church to the castle, carrying suitcases and bags. Somehow he understood they'd spent the night sleeping in the church, head to toe on tight wooden pews, after being brought there late the previous evening.

After a fast click of a moment which he intuitively knew to be not a moment but an hour, these same people emerged calmly from the rear of the castle – the men and boys and children undressed down to their underwear, the women undressed down to their slips. In groups of thirty or so they boarded three large enclosed trucks. The soldiers closed the doors. The drivers started the engines. But the trucks did not move. For a minute or so the boy who was Jurgen thought he could hear the people shouting, but from this distance he could not understand what they said. Then just silence – and the trucks finally rolling away slowly, in the direction of the fires.

In the floating world which was his dream, the picnic continued. The children laughed and played. The ladies sipped lemonade. The men joked and laughed. After a while, following the main feast, several of the servers in pajamas went back to the castle. They returned with musical instruments: a trumpet, a tuba, a french horn. The men in pajamas stood behind the women and began to play. They played bold military marching music which they delivered expertly enough, but with little enthusiasm or strength. Later on there was a cake with candles – for whom he did not at first know. The band rendered "Happy Birthday" while everyone sang. At last he was surprised and delighted to find himself blowing out the candles. Following this, an unsmiling pajama-clad man juggled balls for the delighted children.

In his dream he wanted desperately to see the inside of the castle. He thought it must be grand, like the magical palaces described in fairy stories read to him by his mother. He imagined a vast and wide spiral staircase, the empty armor of long-dead knights standing guard down impossibly long halls, and princes and princesses roving about. Also jesters entertaining the court. But his father said *no*. The castle was not for play. The castle was a serious place. And Jurgen was disappointed.

Near the end of the day the band struck up one last tune while the men and women stood and sang the *Horst Wessel Song*. His uncle, evidently an honored guest, led them all – in command, conducting with his hands.

The sun began to set. The men in pajamas cleared the tables. The smoke of the far-off fires rose again through the day's dimming light. A gentle breeze came up, and with it a whiff of something unpleasant: a strangely soft and delicate rancidness which dissipated as fast as it emerged, and might have been easily ignored. A fragment of unlovely truth which momentarily peaked out from behind a tree, then ran quickly back into the forest, ashamed to show its face.

Jurgen awoke with a start.

Chelmno, he thought. *Now I remember Chelmno.*

*

Kolm had been underground long enough – all these long years, ever since '45 – to feel somewhat confident. Yet he still maintained many precautions. He believed himself safe, yes, but he did not take his safety for granted. His security was a precious and delicate thing, one requiring constant attention: just like the most fragile of flowers. He never fooled himself by thinking he could or should be smug about his so-called "escape." Eichmann grew smug, got sloppy and careless, and it had not gone well for him. Eichmann's lesson was not lost on Kolm. While at his ease and quite comfortable in his adopted identity, Kolm nevertheless always remained vigilant – just like an eagle at rest, ever aware of its surroundings and ready to soar at a second's notice.

Kolm took nothing at face value. He accepted no "generally accepted" wisdom. Not ever. None. Check and double-check, then check once more. *Verification* in all things. Only after verification might trust come. Even then it would be Kolm's own unique brand of trust – a quite jaded and cynical variety tinged with skepticism: an art in which Kolm had come to excel even before puberty.

He'd realized early on he was generally smarter than almost everyone he encountered, whether they be priests or teachers or parents or burgomasters. But instinctively he took pains to keep this intelligence to himself. Was not a revolver hidden beneath a jacket, or a knife stashed in a boot, by nature of more value than the same item laid out on a table for all to see?

Thus he'd been clandestine all his life. And a master of subterfuge. Those who believed themselves his closest intimates were themselves subject to his misdirection and misinformation. His day-to-day life represented a series of obtuse prophylactic measures. Each one of his friends, comrades, and associates knew only what he wanted them to know at any given moment. And to each he often supplied completely different facts as suited his need or whim. Any investigator trying to piece together a picture of Kolm by interrogating his various contacts would find himself confronted not with a portrait, but rather a kaleidoscope of random, nebulous, and often conflicting data.

Not even Ingrid knew his true identity, though she believed she did. His friend and neighbor Winifred Wagner – the unreformed Nazi and grand-dame of the Bayreuth Festival – likewise thought herself the sole confidential carrier of the only true information concerning his actual name and history, all of it divulged in the strictest confidence, and all of it fabricated.

As for the men he helped, they knew him by a dozen different names, believed he lived in a dozen different towns, and made contact with him through a dozen different channels. He was not one person. He was many. He was *Legion*. He was everywhere and nowhere: a ghost of flesh and blood whom some knew in one incarnation, others in another. Any outsider who wanted to find him would have to dance through an enormous hall of mirrors, a funhouse of Kolm's own design, before failing miserably.

Some of his contacts demanded more caution than others. Helga Rath, for all her stunning attributes, was one of these. Publicly, he had no association with her whatsoever. To do so would have, in the long run, been suicide. Indeed, he had never even met her face to face. At least not in his incarnation as Kolm. In general, she was too prominent, too well-known, too involved with self-promotion, too much in the limelight. But then she could afford to be. She was not hunted. She was, as well, useful. She served an important role. A public standard bearer seemed necessary: a beacon to those in need. Not a few of the fugitives to whom he'd given help had come through her referral. It was not as if Kolm could hang out a sign. So, Helga was sometimes a valuable conduit – most recently by bringing this young Enkert to his attention.

*

Ruth sometimes mused about how both she and Jurgen spent inordinate amounts of time kicking about the remnants of German history – she buried under the unwitting testimony of criminals from the modern dark age, he generally (though certainly not this week) trolling through happier artifacts left by more noble and inspired men and women: such things as beautiful furniture, fine art, and rare manuscripts and books. Between them they spanned the breadth of German experience: the two distinct and profoundly opposite poles of German culture and tribal memory. The bad and the good. The hideous and the splendid. The putrid and the sublime. Genocide and Goethe.

And today, once again, her business was genocide as she and Dieter screened still more raw footage:

> *Unnamed Treblinka guard:* They were the real killers, you know, those dirty swine. They knew no bounds, those kapos. They'd do anything to stay alive, for the extra food and the better barracks. To their own people!   And remember, they didn't just do our bidding, the kapos. No. They helped themselves as well. Corruption. Rape. They took women and kept them alive for as long as they wanted, then cast them off. They'd barter food for sex. Some of them would even take little girls, or boys, depending on their inclinations. They were disgusting.

Dieter: And guards never did such things.

Guard: Of course not. We'd never touch Juden. SS? Never! Besides we had our own, a brothel right there with good German girls.

Dieter: But back to the kapos. It is important for people to understand this.

Guard: Yes! They were the epitomy of Jewish deceit, weren't they? And cruel. Such beatings. We guards were disciplined, strategic, pragmatic. We did what we needed in order to maintain order. We maintained the face of author-ity, which often meant the necessity of violent reprisals and cruel actions. This is what was called for to achieve terror, and thereby compliance. But the kapos, they doled out misery for fun – for their own amusement and, I think, to try to impress us guards. You know: Showing us their hearts were in their work. That they were efficient, useful, and should be kept in their jobs. But this was the joke. They were never kept in their jobs. Not for long.

Dieter: No?

Guard: No. See, there were always more trains: more fresh and stronger bodies, more heartless wretches eager to kiss the ass of their enemies, the enemies of their entire race, their jailers. A kapo needed strength. It takes strength to be a brute! Plus, we learned to dislike them intensely. Where killing the others was a job, killing the kapos once we grew tired of them became something of a pleasure. They were always so shocked, those yidds. Each one thought he had it made. Each one thought so long as he kept dancing to our tune we'd let him dance forever.

Dieter: And to cooperate in the destruction of their own people!

Guard: Precisely! Of course, that was the main reason we despised them. Imagine a German – a *real* German – doing that? Never in a thousand years. Never in a million. And look at us even now. Comrades still. We all do what we can, and take risks. We all are there for each other, and ultimately for Germany. When I say this I am talking about the *real* soldiers, you understand, not some weak bureaucrat who was a coward from the start and did nothing but ride a desk. I am talking about us SS who did the actual work. *We* are still loyal – as are many others.

Dieter: And a wonderful example, which I hope this film will show.

Guard: Danke shön!

Dieter: You're welcome.
Guard: You know, I'm sure, many people will hate you, attack you, when

you publish this film. *If you can publish it.*
The Jew-controlled media likes its own
version. So, it is up to people like you
and me, clear-thinking Germans, to con-
front the chaos called *democracy*, and
remind people what a truly rational,
civilized culture looks like. The young
people especially need instruction. Look
at how they are corrupted by all that is
on the radio and television and record
machines. Everywhere you look you see
good German youth dancing like animals to American rock and roll. Nigger
music.

Dieter: Terrible.

Guard: It is not their fault. They have
been trained and propagandized from
the cradle to despise their race, their
history, their heritage. They have been
fed the most distorted stories. They have
been made ashamed, and now cannot
run far enough from their true selves,
their true destiny. They have been cor-

rupted. They need re-education. It will take time. But time is on our side. After all, there's all the time in the world. And all this materialism and hedonism will fall of its own weight. You watch.

Dieter: Tell the story about your brother and the so-called liberation. I've already heard it, but tell it for the camera.

Guard: Well, yes, this shows Germans have no monopoly on so-called war crimes. My brother was stationed at Dachau. He was Waffen-SS, just like me. He'd been wounded by the Russians, and ended up being re-assigned to the camp once he'd recuperated. He was sick with flu at the time the Americans came. He was in the guards' hospital barracks with a number of other guards receiving treatment for this or that. Some were SS. Some were Wehrmacht.

So, anyway, here come the Americans. Helmut – that's my brother, *Helmut* – Helmut went to the door of the hospital waving a white handkerchief. You know, surrender. An American soldier ran up and grabbed him, shoved a machine gun under his chin, and pulled him out onto the ground. Another American went into the hospital and ordered everybody out. There was one SS man too ill to move. The same soldier walked up to where he lay and put a bullet through his head.

After all of the Germans had exited the barracks, the Americans split them up. SS to the right. Wehrmacht to the left. The Americans lined the SS against a wall and mowed them down with machine guns. My brother only survived because when the man next to him was shot my brother made a point of falling with him and getting underneath his body. The dead soldier's blood ran over my brother, making it look like he too was dead. The blood – the good German blood of his fellow SS man – saved him!

Right after this, before the Americans had time to make sure all the SS were actually dead, a bunch of drunken prisoners showed up and distracted the Americans. Believe it or not, the commander of the camp had actually given the keys to the liquor lockers to some of the prisoners before he ran away. Don't ask me why. Later on, the Americans armed these drunkards, who proceeded to murder forty more SS troopers.

Where my brother lay against the wall, he was the only one not dead or severely wounded. Men groaned and wanted to die and shouted to the Americans to please end them. Prisoners came and kicked and spat on them. Then an American medic wearing a Red Cross arm-band came and tossed razor blades at the dying, saying "Take these and finish yourselves off. Enough bullets have been wasted on you." A man to the other side of Helmut slit his one wrist, then handed the blade to Helmut and asked him to do the other. But just at that moment a senior American officer arrived on the scene and ordered the killing stopped. At least the killing by Americans.

Eventually, my brother and a few others were allowed to leave the camp. But they barely got out alive. Later on my brother was arrested and put on trial and executed, like so many others.

So, there are your *humanitarians!* There are your Americans, those allies of the Communists. And there are your "victims," the drunken pigs behaving like animals the first chance they got, the first moment they were let out of their cage.

Who needs more proof than this that all we said was true? There, right there, was the first glimpse of what the post-Reich world was to become, under the disguise of equality and justice and liberty. Mongrels. Free range mongrels. *Bahh!*

*

The man with the eye-patch beneath dark glasses watched from a distance. He never tired of this scene: the old Bayreuth town square surrounded, as it was, by classic 17th and 18th century Bavarian houses and storefronts.

The blonde – on whom he focused most of his attention – sat on a bench in front of the old Mohren Apothecary. Behind her, carved into the apothecary's massive stone front, rose a large gold-gilded griffin with the legs, body, and tail of a lion, and the head, wings, and talons of an eagle. *Majestic*, he thought, *majestic, proud, and powerful – the king of beasts combined with the king of birds to create the traditional guardian of the Divine.* The builders of past centuries surely knew how to merge art with architecture, while the builders of today knew nothing but right angles, flat surfaces, and budgets. He personally despised stark, unornamented functionality – all that Bauhaus "form follows function" bullshit. *Beauty first*, he thought. *Beauty first above all things.*

Tourists walked across the square, snapping pictures and delighting in the Bavarian quaintness of the vast space. Men and women neatly dressed in business clothes walked to or from offices, buses, and trains. Students wearing God knows what moved toward the university campus with their backpacks and book-bags. Fat men wearing white aprons stood behind food carts, the steam from their carts rising and wafting through the air. In the far distance, a mime contorted himself within the constraints of an invisible box. Pigeons alighted here and there, racing each other for crumbs. Two yawning police officers strolled casually about the square in long, lazy loops, sleepily vigilant for the type of discontent or thievery which rarely occurred here.

The man with the eye-patch beneath dark glasses could not help but notice how all the men and all the boys furtively ogled the blonde in her skimpy halter, abbreviated shorts, and pumps. He knew Ingrid enjoyed the attention – got a kick out of turning eyes, putting herself on display, making an exhibition. She was, after all, a true Nordic beauty. Evolution's work of art. He would not argue. Neither would she.

They'd each been in their places a half hour already, having arrived purposely early. This was what one did. *Tradecraft,* as George Smiley would call it. Or simply being careful. Whatever. The point was he'd spotted no one besides himself lurking about the edges or – except for the tourists, the bored cops, the absurd mime, or the men with white aprons – spending too much time here. He spied no-one else doing as he and Ingrid did: simply loitering. This made him able to relax. Not that he was ever *totally* able to relax. The world had too many sharp edges for that.

It was another ten minutes before the young man wearing the red sweater entered the square and made straight for Ingrid in her spot before the apothecary. He strode at a vigorous gait, his back straight, his arms swinging at his sides. Almost soldier-like. Very good. The man with the eyepatch beneath dark glasses watched as Ingrid and the young man smiled, shook hands, and exchanged a few worlds. Ingrid then rose, took him by the arm, and led him out of the square, down the several blocks toward the mansion.

The man with the eyepatch beneath dark glasses strode a block or so behind them, his hands in his pockets. Once the two had entered the mansion, he lingered across the street, smoking a cigarette, taking note of the pedestrians passing by. He was pleased to discern nothing extraordinary. Once his cig had burned down to the filter he threw it to the ground, crushed it under his heel, and proceeded to the house.

He found Ingrid and the young man sitting in the living room.

"Jurgen Enkert," he said, removing his glasses.

He spoke in a reserved, business-like tone.

He walked to where the young man sat, and shook his hand firmly.

"I am Kolm. Heinz Kolm."

"A pleasure, Mr. Kolm. Thank you for seeing me."

Kolm sat down on a large upholstered chair across from the couch.

"Jurgen was just telling me he's never been to Bayreuth before," said Ingrid.

"No? A pity. This city is a truly splendid relic of another time. A relic largely unscathed by the war, I'm happy to say."

"This house right here is really something," said Jurgen.

"Yes. 17th century. 1652 to be exact. Just one of many beautiful places Bayreuth has to offer – a feast of some of the best baroque and rococo architecture in the world, you know. But then it is no surprise you appreciate such things, given your studies. I've lived here a very long time. This particular house, you may be interested to learn, was the childhood home of Johann Philipp Heinel. In fact, he was born in what is now my bedroom, in 1800. I'm sure you must be familiar with his work."

"Indeed. A master. A student of Langer, I believe. Wonderful historical paintings, portraits, genre subjects, and landscapes. A great breadth of activity. I especially like his landscapes with figures."

Jurgen suddenly realized why Kreigsman and Rubin had insisted his adopted profile be as close as possible in background to his real profile. Any expertise or knowledge he demonstrated went to bolster confidence in the truth of his fraudulent history.

"Have you by chance done any restorations of his works?" asked Kolm.

"No, not at all. I'm not even sure, to be honest, whether we even have any of his paintings at the National Gallery. It is such a massive collection." That was true enough. He hadn't a clue.

Kolm turned his head and looked about the large living room, as if seeing it for the first time.

"I love buildings which contain history, buildings with a *past*. Modern structures seem so ... so soulless. They tend to be mere boxes – *containers* for human life. No better than a freight car or a barracks. How people can maintain their sanity in such cubes is beyond me."

"Agreed."

Ingrid treated Jurgen to a wry smile. He wondered if her boss realized she'd booked him into just such
a monstrosity – the modern but very comfortable
Atlantia. He guessed not. And it seemed as though
Ingrid somehow enjoyed the subversive irony.

"I envy you your job at the National Gallery.
Imagine, to be surrounded by such wonders and excellence every day. It must hardly seem like work."

"One does not get rich, of course."

"No, but one eats and sleeps and spends his days
doing what he loves," said Kolm. "That is the real
wealth. Remember, just a blink of an eye we are all in
the ground. Mere money remains behind. One only
needs so much."

"Still – and I hope you do not mind my saying so
– this is certainly not the home of a poor man."

Kolm smiled.

"You're right. I've been lucky here and there; yet
I'm happy to say financial gain has never been a
priority with me. I try to spend my time on higher,
more meaningful, more noble pursuits. Nevertheless I
have, as I say, been lucky along the way."

Ingrid stood.

"I will leave you gentlemen to your conversation.
I have some work to do."

Once Ingrid had left the room, Kolm took out a cigarette and lit it. Kolm took a long drag on the cigarette, tilted his head back, and exhaled the smoke in a slow, casual stream up toward the ceiling. Then he turned back to Jurgen.

"Your agenda has been explained to me."

"Good."

"I do not know your father, but I am sorry to hear he is unwell."

Jurgen nodded.

"And this is why he has returned? His health?"

Jurgen nodded again.

"It is very dangerous for him," said Kolm. "I'm surprised he did not just do his doctoring wherever he's been all these years."

"He really is not doing doctoring. He says he is going to die. His return is, so far as I can tell, an act of nostalgia. He wants to die in Germany. And out of this same sense of nostalgia he wants to find his brother."

"I see."

Kolm seemed to become deeply contemplative. He stared off into space for half a minute or so before being interrupted by Jurgen.

"Do you mind my asking you something, Herr Kolm?"

"Not at all. I will answer if I can. Proceed."

"I've been told you are in a position to help me. Are you, yourself, a veteran?"

Kolm smiled.

"No, sad to say. I have a heart murmur which caused me to not pass the physical for either the SS or the Wehrmacht. But this is also why I may – and I emphasize, *may* – be in a position to be of assistance. With a 'clean' *jacket* – as the Americans call it – I never drew much scrutiny in the early days after the war, and still do not now. I have nothing to hide or run from. I have no suspicious history. Thus I am somewhat more free than others to assist comrades in various ways."

"I understand and I'm grateful."

"A lot of people look at this eye-patch and assume it is a war wound," said Kolm. "Nothing so glamorous, I'm afraid. A simple traffic accident several years ago."

Jurgen nodded.

"I've been informed of all you know about your uncle: that he may have escaped to Italy, and so forth. You understand, of course, there are no formal records anywhere which one might consult on this topic. So any revelation I might have for you is purely anecdotal. You are correct to assume that if your uncle is alive, he has every reason to be as obscure as possible. All that most comrades can say *for certain* is that not since the war has he been active or even *present* in what we might call our *community*, whether here or abroad. Of course, were he dead, he'd be quite anonymously so wherever he ended up."

"This all seems clear."

"That being said," Kolm continued, "I have made a few inquiries with a few contacts, and I have come up with an answer for you. A sad answer, I'm afraid, and an anecdotal answer, but one which I believe to be true."

"Yes?"

"Your uncle died while trying to escape over the mountains to Italy in '45. I have spoken directly to a comrade who says he was with him, and claims to have helped bury him. Your uncle reportedly came down with typhus during the trek, and the typhus killed him. The man who was with your uncle is himself, to this day, incommunicado. He does not recall the precise location of the grave. He does not know those mountains. They were being led by a guide."

Jurgen pretended to digest this for a moment, as if stunned and saddened by news which he knew now with vast sudden certainty – like a blessed, revelatory wave rolling over him – to be a lie.

"My father shall be very upset by this."

"I'm sure. May I make a suggestion? To relieve you of the burden, why not allow me to send a few of our local Munich comrades to your father, to explain to him? I will also ask them to look out for him – you know, in his last illness. You, I imagine, must get back to London. To your life. To your job. It will be a reassurance for you that your father is in good hands. It seems the least I can do. We are here to help each other, after all."

"That is very kind of you. Indeed I have to get back to London directly. I won't really have time for another Munich stop. I was planning to simply call my father with whatever news I got."

Kolm shook his head.

"The telephone is no good for this type of thing. As I said, I'll dispatch some friends. It will be better."

"*Donka*," said Jurgen. "You are very kind. I will do as you say. I will get back to my life."

"Yes, and we will phone you and keep you posted on your father's status. This I promise."

They did not speak much longer before Jurgen took his leave.

Kolm rang a bell to summon Ingrid, who showed Jurgen out. Once Jurgen was safely out the door, Kolm removed the eye-patch. He'd been dying to do that. Damned itchy thing. But it was quite remarkable how such a simple adjustment could dramatically change one's features.

Jurgen, in turn, congratulated himself on his calm and self-control. How well he had contained and conducted himself despite his revelation; his sudden and unexpected flash of recognition. Now he walked as fast as he could to his hotel so he could telephone Kreigsman and give him news which would make the man very glad. Then, in triumph, he would head home.

*

Many kilometers away, in a seedy one-room loft apartment on the outskirts of Bonn, a former Auschwitz camp guard sat in the dark and worried.

On the table before him rested a bottle of whiskey and a glass. The bottle had been full when he'd started a half hour before, but was now nearly empty. The man who had once been named Troper but who now was Waldheim – Carl Waldheim – poured himself another.

Waldheim asked (and, he admitted, *received*) very little from life. His tiny apartment contained not much more than a bed, a card-table, three folding chairs, a bureau, and a television placed atop a milk crate. His wardrobe in his one small closet consisted of only a few cheap items, and these hardly new. But he was secure in his spartan, aesthetic existence. Kolm saw to that. Kolm covered his rent, and gave him his monthly stipend. For this he was available, on call, to do whatever Kolm might ask. And he was happy to do so.

Sometimes this simply meant receiving a parcel from Kolm in Bayreuth, repacking the item, and remailing it from a Bonn post office. Sometimes it meant meeting strangers in parks and handing off packets filled with who knew what, also from Kolm. Sometimes it meant something more sinister.

He'd followed orders, hadn't he? Yes. Of course. As always, he'd marched on without a single question. In concert with the Confessor and the fat man he'd vetted and armed and trained the men. He'd purchased the two vans which would ferry them to and from the scene. He'd arranged the false registrations for the vehicles. He'd obtained the fraudulent passports and exit visas for the shooters, and arranged their escapes by commercial flights to places as near or far as Sicily or Chile.

Some of them were comrades simply in need of a change of scenery, and utterly reliable. Some were the Confessor's equally committed – though thoroughly mad – holy zealots. Others were just guns for hire – mercenaries without ideology, without principle. They bore watching. They would not be fully briefed until just shortly before the "action." But he knew them all to be capable: the comrades because of their histories of service and unflinching loyalty to the Reich, the religionists because they were fanatics, and the hired guns because of their resumes: merciless apprenticeships in the killing fields of Cambodia and the Congo.

The mission itself could not be more simple. Carnage – pure, irredeemable carnage. Brutal punishment. No survivors. Only bodies and blood to tell the tale. Carcasses left where there once had been faith. A tomb left where there once had been hope. The ruthlessness and devastation of the camps brought to the very house of the Hebrew God, who – as before – could offer no protection. The chosen people were to be mowed down and slaughtered in the very midst of their prayers. Their appeals to the Father were to be answered with nothing but a bombardment of tossed grenades and frantic machine gun fire. The grotesque stunned masks of the dead: how alike they would be to the faces on the piles at Auschwitz and Treblinka. Those faces would show the world history was not over. Just interrupted.

But he was worried. It had happened so quickly during his routine surveillance of the synagogue. His surprise and confusion at seeing the young filmmaker emerge from the place could not be overstated. Along with the young man came a pretty brunette, an older gray-haired lady, and a little boy of perhaps four or five.

Waldheim followed for several blocks. He watched them turn into a large gray apartment building, then waited a few minutes before entering the vestibule. He noted ten mailboxes. Kruger, Keltenberg, Roth, and others, with just one standing out: *Ha-Shoa Films, GbR,* beneath which were scribbled the names "Jurgen & Ruth Todt."

As he stood there an elderly woman stepped into the vestibule, about to depart the building. She dragged a shopping cart on wheels behind her. Waldheim

moved to pretend he was just leaving as well. He held
the outer door for the old lady to get through.

"*Danka!*" she said. "It is nice some of us still have
manners!"

"My pleasure," he answered. "I take it you live
here."

"Yes. A very long time. Over twenty-five years!
But I don't recognize you."

"I've just been visiting a friend."

"Who?"

"Todt."

"Oh yes, such nice people. Jurgen and that pretty
Ruth, the movie-maker. And such a sweet little boy."

"Ruth is very talented," he ventured.

"Yes! You know she and her assistant, that Dieter,
they even interviewed *me* for their movie. I was not
liking the way my hair looked and I was just in a
house-dress, but Ruth said not to worry. These things
don't matter. My one chance to be a movie-star and I
look like a witch!"

She laughed as she said it.

"And why did she interview you?"

"Well, of course, I was in Sobidor, don't you
know. I'm a survivor. She wanted to know all about
it. And it was hard for me. I don't usually talk about

those things. But Ruth insisted I bear witness, and tell my story. She was right. I did it once and never again. Now anyone who wants to hear about those sad things can just go see me in my movie."

"Quite a project she has going."

"Well, her heart is in it, as I'm sure you know. She is a good Jew. Her parents were lost. She was just a child of course. She got saved by family friends, Christians. But her parents are gone. Poof!"

"That young Dieter who works with her seems quite professional."

"Yes, Dieter," the old woman said. "Dieter Ohlendorf. So nice. He is here often. He helped me move my couch. I'm no good at these things any more. I can always ask him, or Jurgen, when I need assistance."

"Ruth's husband."

"Yes, Jurgen."

"Well, have a good day," he said as they reached the corner. "I'm turning here."

"Yes, you too. It is so nice to chat with new friends."

"Indeed."

He came to a phone booth two blocks on. After stepping inside, he checked the fat directory which hung beneath the phone and found the listing for *Ohlendorf, Dieter*. He made note of the address. He'd visit Dieter this evening. Then he'd get out of town. Screw the Yom Kippur project and screw everything else. That Dieter had him on film, which was bad enough on its own. But if his comrades ever found out, it would be even worse. Time to disappear from everyone forever.

Chapter 6

Wilfried felt he was not only making amends for his race, but also for his Church.

Yes, a large number of Righteous Gentiles had actively opposed and sought to subvert the Third Reich – particularly its genocide of the Jews and so many others. But many more so-called Christians – including many practicing Catholics – had served as functionaries of the Holocaust, and done so all too willingly. Even more inexcusable had been the silence and inaction of the Church as an institution. Wilfried, with his scholar's eye, had made a deep and sad study of the matter.

Eugene Pacelli – the man who became Pope Pius XII in 1939 – effectively did nothing to save European Jewery from its fate. Having inherited an ancestral antipathy toward Jews as "the killers of Christ," Pacelli as Vatican Secretary of State played a key role in negotiating the Reich Concordat of 1933, which protected the Church in Germany in exchange for the Church's silence on political matters. In effect, this killed-off the Catholic Centrist Party which at the time offered Hitler his only remaining significant political opposition. This party had previously been successful in rolling back Bismarck's Kulturkampf, and had steadily and openly opposed the rise of Nazism – including even refusing the Host to party members. With the Concordat, the autonomy of the German Catholic hierarchy became a thing of the past, as did that hierarchy's ability to speak out against Hitler without acting in violation of Vatican authority.

Subsequently, under Pius as Pope, the Vatican maintained diplomatic relations with the Reich throughout the war. Pius failed even to protest the round-ups of Roman Jews, despite the fact that these occurred right under his very windows, at the foot of Vatican Hill. Indeed, throughout that dark period, it was Pius's abject silence in the face of countless atrocities which went a long way towards sealing the fate of European Jewry. This could not be denied.

Never – not once – did there come from Pius any form of public confrontation, criticism, or plea for justice in the midst of the ongoing Final Solution. But had this been a surprise? After all, the language of Pacelli's own Reich Concordat, even though it called for Germany to protect the rights and lives of Jews who converted to Catholicism, went on to charac-terize the fate of other German Jews as solely an "internal affair" of the Reich – a topic on which the Vatican claimed no right to comment.

It was the actions of many right-thinking members of the Church – the *people*, the real *body* of the Church as opposed to the monolithic bureaucratic institution – which at least partially redeemed Catholics and Catholicism with regard to the Holocaust. Here were the saints and heroes. The German Jesuits who hid Jews in their cellars. The monks who led refugees over mountains, through valleys, and across borders. The countless couples who, like Wilfried and his wife, harbored Jewish children disguised as their own. And the priests who spoke out and were killed immediately for doing so, as well as those who went to die in the camps.

Yes, these were the truly righteous. But there were also other Catholics who without hesitation marched women and children to their deaths as a daily drill, brutally herded families out of boxcars with a viciousness one would not otherwise inflict on cattle, and did all they could to keep the wheels of death turning right up until the very end.

The irony? When Wilfried prayed, he did so neither for the righteous nor for the murdered; in the end it was only the murderers who needed prayer.

The others did not. That's the way sin and redemption worked. Thus he prayed for the SS, for any and all clergy or lay-people who participated through action or inaction, and for Pacelli.

The perpetrators truly needed prayer. But they also needed killing.

*

Jurgen and Ruth woke neither early nor enthusiastically. With Eli spending the night at Lisel's, Jurgen and Ruth had focused on their reunion. Again and again she'd welcomed him home. They were both still dead asleep at noon. The sound of a large truck passing and several backfires of its engine finally roused them.

Jurgen watched from his pillow as Ruth rose, naked, and walked to the bathroom. She emerged a few minutes later wearing a robe.

"That," he sighed, "was marvelous."

"I rather enjoyed myself as well."

"Maybe, I should go away more often."

"No, I don't think so."

Ruth sat down on the edge of the bed. She ran her fingers through her long hair, pushing it back over her shoulders.

"And what is our agenda today?" he asked. "You working?"

"No. Dieter has another interview to tend to. He'll do the shoot today and the processing tonight, and then come over tomorrow to show me the rough cut. We'll talk on the phone later this afternoon I suppose. Eli will be with Lisel until after dinner, then one of us will go get him. I believe she plans to bring him to the Natural History Museum to see the dinosaur bones. He always likes that."

"*All* little boys like that. She used to take me there too."

"You see? You gave her good practice for Eli."

"Indeed I did. In fact, that was my plan all along."

"Yes. I'm sure! You saw the future so clearly even at age eight."

"True, even though it is hard to believe."

Ruth rolled her eyes.

"And what about you?" she asked. "How do you intend to be productive this afternoon?"

"I'm going to get a piece out of storage, the Chinese chest I bought a few weeks ago, and send it off to Sotheby's. They've given me a good auction estimate. So, I'll get it packed and going."

Ruth nodded.

"How about some breakfast? Eggs? Pancakes?"

"Yes, pancakes would be wonderful."

"Alright. You shower and I'll fix us up."

As Jurgen stepped into the shower he reflected on how relaxed he felt, but also how satisfied. He'd done what had been asked and done it as best he could. He wondered how productive the whole exercise would be in the end; but no matter what happened he'd at least made his contribution. This was important, even if only a small circle knew it. This alone was worth any price he'd paid.

It seemed strange, ironic, and up-side-down that in being Jurgen Enkert – his technically "true" identity – he'd had to shed his real and actual self, Jurgen Todt. He'd dearly love to have the luxury of living without any mask of any kind. He did not like secrets, even the most innocent ones. He knew they had a way of festering and turning malignant over time – of growing beyond themselves and becoming impossible to maintain. This went for all secrets, even inherited ones.

He did not plan to see his father again. There would be no point. Spiritually and psychologically they could not be further away from each other, even though the old man had no hint of this and, after

Jurgen's Academy Award-winning performance, thought them bonded. The only contact information he'd given his father was the fraudulent London phone number; this would no longer exist once the work was done, successful or not. And until then an answering machine would do its job.

Still, he enjoyed fantasizing what it would be like were the old bigot informed about his Jewish daughter-in-law and, worse, Jewish grandson. What would the old man's reaction be? Rage, shame – both? Or would he quietly assimilate it, fatalistically, as just one more defeat and indignity to be silently endured by a broken old soldier awaiting the deliverance of death. Perhaps the latter. Yes, given his father's current mood – most certainly.

As he soaped and rinsed himself, Jurgen imagined he was washing away the slime of the people he'd encountered over the past several days, as if their sins and blasphemies might be somehow communicable and he needed to guard against catching whatever disease made them what they were. He felt as though he needed to ritualistically purify himself for re-entry into the the light of day – his genuine life. As a more practical and real way of doing this, he resolved to attend confession and late afternoon mass, and to take the Host, once he'd gotten the Sotheby's shipment out of the way. Then he'd pick up Eli from Lisel's.

*

Jurgen and Ruth were just about to sit down to their late breakfast when the phone rang. Not more than a half hour later, they sat stunned and shocked on the couch in Dieter's apartment, watching as a police medical examiner wearing surgical gloves layed Dieter's body out on a plastic sheet and then – in a detached, professional voice – elaborated the cold physical facts of torture. The medical examiner's assistant stood nearby with a pad and pencil, taking notes.

"Multiple stab wounds but death from asphyxiation with plastic bag. Evidence of torture through burning of fingers, toes, genitals, and slicing of skin. Four swastika symbols carved on stomach, upper torso, and both facial cheeks. Also severe bruising from blunt force trauma to the head, face, and stomach ..."

Once the examiner had finished his analysis, he and his assistant placed Dieter's corpse into a black body bag, zipped it up tight, and unceremoniously heaved it onto a gurney.

"Those tight stairs are going to be a bitch," said the assistant as he grabbed the handle nearest the head.

The examiner grunted. "Just our luck."

The two ghouls were hardly gone a minute, loudly rattling down the stairs, and cursing all the while, before a young, burly detective – gruff, and seemingly unaffected – came to stand before Jurgen and Ruth.

"He was your friend?" he asked, addressing himself to Ruth.

"Yes," she answered.

"Boyfriend?"

"*No!* Friend, and colleague."

"Colleague?"

"We are filmmakers. We were – we *are* – making a documentary."

"About what?"

"The Holocaust."

The detective pondered this for a moment.

"Given the way this was done, I'm thinking maybe somebody doesn't like your topic."

Ruth nodded.

"He'd been interviewing former SS. His father was in the SS and was executed by the Allies after the war. Dieter posed as a neo-Nazi, sympathetic to their side of the story. We've been trying to catch old SS men off-guard you see, talking about things they wouldn't normally, and being honest. Dieter told them he would keep their interviews confidential until the time was right to inspire German youth – long after the interviewees were dead. We wanted – *want* – to expose them, you see, as zealots then and zealots now. That's the idea."

"Evidently a very dangerous idea," said the detective. "He wasn't a Jew?"

"No."

"And you are a Jew?"

"Yes."

"Well, I suppose maybe one of his interview subjects wasn't quite so stupid as you and he figured. I would guess somebody realized what was going on. That would be my hunch. That would seem, at this point, to be the most obvious explanation. I must say I think you are both very foolish. Some of these people can be quite dangerous still. Your friend played with fire, you understand."

Jurgen hoped the detective was not trying to make some terrible pun based on Dieter's wounds, which included numerous burns. He found the degree of the man's coldness and insolence unnerving, and suspicious.

"Do you," the detective asked, "have information regarding to whom he'd spoken or to whom he'd planned to speak? Is there a list?"

Ruth nodded.

"Yes. Back at my apartment. I will give it to you."

"Very good. The original, if you please, and any copies. I cannot have that list floating around while the investigation is ongoing. You understand?"

"Yes."

The detective sat back and turned his eyes toward Jurgen.

"And you. What is your story? You are her husband?"

"Yes."

"You make films too?"

"No, I deal in antiques."

"Here in Bonn."

"Yes."

"Maybe your wife should go into the antiques business. Maybe it is safer."

Jurgen shrugged. He thought the observation uncalled-for. He decided he really did not like this man. Too smug. Too superior. He supposed the police

saw so much horror they simply had to remain disen-
gaged, or else go crazy. But this detective conveyed
something beyond mere disengagement: an attitude
of utter remorselessness which Jurgen thought disturbing. And objectionable. He did not trust the man.
He decided not to divulge anything further, not right
now, no matter how possibly relevant.

"Well," said the detective. "We will take your list
and see what can be done. But I am not sure we will
be able to come up with an answer. Perhaps we'll get
lucky. Who knows?"

It did not seem he cared much one way or the
other.

"I just hope my wife is safe," said Jurgen.

"Was your dead friend telling his interviewees
with whom he was working?"

Ruth shook her head in the negative.

"Then I think you must be OK. If I thought there
was a risk I would put a watch on you. But we are
very short of men, short of resources. I cannot waste
them."

Waste? Jurgen did not care for the response, but
did not argue.

"I will send one of my men around later for that
list," continued the detective, "so we can get started

digging. Then just wait to hear from us. I will keep you posted."

"*Donka,*" said Ruth.

"You can leave now," he said.

He'd hardly uttered that last word before he'd turned his back to them and begun to talk quietly with one of his subordinates.

Having been dismissed – and yes, Jurgen thought that the word to use – he and Ruth walked out of the apartment and down the stairs: the same stairs which the medical examiner and his assistant had found so inconvenient.

"How horrible," said Ruth as they walked up the street. "I just can't digest it. All of this seems so surreal. Poor Dieter. How they made him suffer. I could hardly recognize him. They turned him from a person into a thing, a grotesque and pitiful thing. Dehumanized. And some sadist took pure delight out of doing it. You can tell, can't you? There's no mistaking."

"Yes."

Jurgen knew he should just let her rant, get it out, and he did.

"Beasts. Animals. Maybe evil isn't quite so banal after all. Maybe it is ambitious, hungry, energetic."

Based on what he'd seen and experienced over the past several days, Jurgen had to agree. But he did not say so.

Back at Dieter's apartment, the detective turned to a colleague and said: "Fucking Jews. All these years later and still they can't just let things be."

*

Kolm thought about his conversation with young Enkert the previous morning. A pity – truly – he would not be able to help the young man.

He filled two overnight bags. He packed several sweaters and pants and all the usual accoutrements for a few days away. He did not know quite how long he would be gone, or even his eventual itinerary. He'd see how things went. He had decisions to make.

Of course, the timing of young Enkert's arrival, and the timing of the news he brought, could not have been more inconvenient. Such important business as that in which he, the Confessor, and Pechstein found themselves currently engaged did not come along very often.

The organization had always been such a cautious beast, brooding in shadows – an enterprise of hiding and furtive retreat rather than activism and advancement. Seemingly toothless. Seemingly claw-less. Demonstrating strength only at times which demanded strength in order to enforce secrecy and safety. A wounded lion rather than a strong, brave, and hungry one.

Now – their small group agreed – was the time to begin, if ever so slowly, to stake a claim to the late modern era and embrace the future. Now was the time to stop looking backward, and start looking for-ward – before they and other comrades were too old and too slow to do so. Now was the time to recognize the Fatherland as occupied territory in need of liberation.

The planning, financing, and training had taken more than a year, with Pechstein – of the highest rank among them – giving his tacit blessing for the start of preliminary planning. And now, when at last they had Pechstein's final approval, who comes along but young, well-meaning Enkert and his broken, tedious father?

Never mind. Kolm would tend to this thing. But he certainly didn't need this damn diversion. Kolm's devotion to detail, his constant and often productive worrying over minutiae, demanded time for medi-tation and study. He did not think well and clearly when rushed. Who did? And here was a moment calling for the most careful calculations. The most rational thinking. All the more reason to deal quickly and decisively with the Enkert matter, and the threat it posed – get it out of the way lest it become too large and prolonged a distraction.

In addition to packing his bags, Kolm donned a shoulder holster holding a .38. Then he went to a box in one of his bedside drawers and grabbed a handful of bullets. He placed these in a pocket of his Ralph Lauren jacket.

Studying himself in the full-length mirror which hung on the back of his closet door, he observed that he looked quite good for his age. Debonair, sharp, virile: a fit, accomplished gentleman full of confidence, aesthetic wisdom, and *joie de vivre*. He'd made something of himself, and yet remained true to what mattered. He was loyal, and could hold his head up.

Kolm carried both bags downstairs, walked to the rear of the house, and set them down by the kitchen door.

Ingrid sat at the kitchen table, a cup of coffee before her and the newspaper spread out. She was naked under a robe.

"A trip?" she asked.

"Yes. Business."

She knew not to ask where or what, or for how long. Kolm never answered such questions.

"Coffee before you go?"

"Please."

Kolm sat. Ingrid poured from a cannister on the table.

"You will check-in, of course?"

"Yes, yes. Although I'm expecting nothing urgent to arise. Just use the usual script for anyone asking after me, and leave messages with the service."

Ingrid nodded.

He'd not briefed her on the pending event. It was *need to know.*

Kolm admired her efficiency and reliability. Still, as excellent as she was, he harbored no sentimentality about the girl. If she disappeared tomorrow it would be tremendously inconvenient, but nothing more than that.

He'd never been overly sentimental about anyone. Not that he could recall. He realized some people would think this a character flaw, or perhaps even a sickness. He, however, simply thought it effective, expedient, pragmatic. He'd been wired this way for as long as he could remember. Ever since boyhood.

He finished his coffee and stood to leave.

"Alright," he said, opening the rear door and grabbing his bags. "I will call you."

"Very good. See you."

Kolm descended the steps to the alley. His two cars sat under a shed: the Rolls and the BMW. He took the BMW, which he'd long ago registered to his second alias and his lodge address in the Black Forest. The registration in the glove compartment matched the ID he carried in his wallet. His Kolm IDs sat locked in his office safe – for which not even Ingrid knew the combination.

Kolm turned over the engine and fed a tape into the eight-track. Johann Strauss, the younger. *Tales from the Vienna Woods*. He kept the windows closed and put the air-conditioner on low. Roaring up the alley, he turned left at the outlet, toward the highway.

The music would help him think. Not about *what* to do. That could not be more obvious. No, the question he needed to meditate on was how to go about his errand. How to accomplish his task in the most safe and clean way possible.

Some tasks were ones you chose at your own discretion. Others chose you: thrust upon you by fortune, by events out of your control. This job was the latter. It would take him at least four hours to reach his destination, travelling west through Nuremberg, Ingolstadt, and beyond.

Ingrid watched Kolm pull away. She was glad to see him go. She was *always* glad to see him go. From the amount of luggage he carried, she guessed he'd be gone at least two nights. Good. She had her secrets too. And she'd make her plans accordingly.

*

Unedited "Rouch Cut" interview from Ruth Todt's unfinished documentary:

Dieter: So, explain that.

Woman formerly known as Herta Rinkel: Well, you ask do I regret, or do I think it a mistake, that I was a guard at Ravensbrück and other places. To this I say *no.* If anything, I regret that such places existed. *This* was the mistake: that such places ever came to be. But *I* made no mistake. I was assigned. I was conscripted. I was ordered. Had I refused to go to the camps as a guard, I would have been sent there as a prisoner. I am alive here today, and *that* is no mistake! I was only in my early twenties. I wanted to live.

Dieter: Now, I mean no disrespect here in this next question. But for the record we must clear the air on certain points and address what has been said in the biased and one-sided history books. That is the whole point of this film.

Herta: I understand. Go on. I will not be offended.

Dieter: Very well. When you were at Stutthof, before Ravensbrück, the prisoners reportedly gave you the nickname "Herta the Merciless" because of what were allegedly your frequent beatings of the women under your control. Please give me your side.

Herta: Well, I never heard that description until after everything was over. Obviously, this is not a thing which would have been spoken to my face at the time. So I can't tell you whether that name is a post-war invention – an attempt at drama – or not. But yes, it was necessary, the beatings. We were commanded. We'd been trained to do this, you see. In order to maintain discipline. As well, we *had* to display a certain amount of ruthlessness lest our superiors not be pleased. Was I more ruthless than others? I can't say. But I *will* say this: Had I not been the one with the baton or the whip, someone else would have been. These things were *going* to happen, regardless of my participation. Since there were inevitably going to be beatings, I knew which side of the beatings I wanted to be on. We are talking about survival.

Dieter: I can anticipate your answer, but please also speak to me about the so-called "death march" from Ravensbrück to Bergen-Belsen.

Herta: Yes, that was in January or February of '45. It was necessary, because they'd developed a shortage of workers over there at the other camp. "Death march" is not correct. They say now that we were trying to kill the women, brutalize them, make them starve and freeze to death. Nonsense. We wanted to get them to their destination alive. They were *needed.* We just had no transport. Also not much food had been allocated, and the prisoners were not dressed well. Then the snows came. It was out of our hands. We'd been given a schedule. When someone showed they could not make the march, they had to be left. And wasn't it kinder to shoot them than leave them to freeze? And it was a good example to set for the rest, as we had to keep them moving. Also, by weeding out the sick and slow we enabled the whole group to move faster, for their sake as well as ours. We worked with what we had. We guards were not particularly comfortable either, you know!

Dieter: Of course. Now tell me about once you got where you were going.

Herta: The need was for wood cutters and haulers, for people to go into the woods every day and get fuel for the stoves. That was the job. I supervised about sixty of them. Once again, discipline had to be maintained. And this was what we did.

Dieter: Tell me about when the Allies came.

Herta: Ugh. Disgusting. It is in all the films. I'm sure you've seen them. They made us take the corpses of prisoners from the piles and carry them to big open graves dug with bull-dozers. They refused even to let us wear gloves.

I was afraid I'd get typhus. Especially since some of the bodies, well, they'd been in the pile for quite a while and were in a condition where when you picked them up, well, the arms or legs would just tear off. Tell me, what was the point of this display? The same bull-dozers could have pushed the whole pile into the trench in under a minute. This was all for the cameras. *All for the cameras.*

Dieter: How did you escape?

Herta: It was strangely easy. I'm still amazed. I think it was God showing me the way. Quite honestly, I do.

Dieter: Yes?

Herta: We were all still at Bergen-Belsen, incarcerated there in a barracks for several months after the Allies came. I rose in the night and asked the guard permission to use the latrine, which was

out of sight from where he sat. I knew
the camp better than any of those
newcomers. They all thought they had it
sealed up tight, but I knew an almost
secret gate which we'd used to bring in
the wood. I walked well beyond the
latrine in the dark, and out to that gate
which – as I'd guessed – sat unguarded
and unlocked. Then I just kept right on
walking.

After a few miles I stole some
clothes off a wash-line. It was a farm. I
found a shovel and buried my uniform.
I kept walking for a great many days
and nights. I went into the farm fields
and ate ripe fruit and vegetables while
continuing onward, not really sure of
my destination. Eventually I applied for
an identity card. There were so many
refugees. The cards were easy to get and
you could tell them any name you liked.
I used the name of a camp inmate whom
I knew to be dead. That is still my name
today. A few years ago I received a letter
from a woman who thought she'd found

her sister. I did not know what to do. I didn't respond. I changed my address.

Dieter: Were you ever able to get back to your own people?

Herta: Mine is a Hamburg family. I settled here in Bonn and did not contact them for a very long time – almost two years – because I was afraid. Then I could no longer wait and I took the risk and wrote a note. They were so happy. They'd thought I was dead. It was like a resurrection. They came to visit me and eventually, as time passed, I grew confident and was able to visit them. But I like Bonn. It has been my home now for many years. I'd been a nurse before conscription, and have been a nurse again all these years. In the maternity ward. So lovely to be able to help bring such happiness. New life.

Dieter: Any other thoughts before we stop? I want you to have your say.

Herta: Well, only this. I did not hate these women. I did not despise them. I did not think them subhuman, like so many others said they were. I was simply in a situation – well, politics out of our control had put us *all* in the same situation: the captors and the captives, the guards and the guarded. None of us had a choice. As I said before, had I not been on one side of the beatings, I would have been on the other. And that is why I have no guilt. I did what was necessary to get through.

*

Kolm found the seedy neighborhood, the seedy street, and finally the seedy building. It was early afternoon. He parked his car directly outside the half-ruined and much-neglected tenement, and made sure to lock the doors behind him before he began up the steps. He carried with him a bottle of whiskey and a bag of food.

Poverty. Urchins small and large, young and

elderly, haunted the street like idle spirits lost between Heaven and Hell, but much closer to the latter. Tawdry, near-ancient streetwalkers – the lowest tier of that profession – cruised forlornly back and forth. The street might have been named *Desolation* or *Purgatory* rather than *Potsdamer Platz*, although *Potsdamer* seemed not too far off the mark either: the city where the butchers Truman, Churchill, and Stalin once gathered to carve up conquered Germany. How appropriate: This no-man's land of the soul bereft of culture, dignity, hope.

The residents of this destitute place lived under the rule of no authority other than circumstance: that most maleable of all possible dictators under which only the weak and stupid might buckle and feel conquered. Whoever made their so-called life here had volunteered for it, and deserved nothing better.

These might be Aryans, but certainly the very poorest variety, and a disgrace. Traitors to their cultural and biological inheritance. Outliers. *Auslanders* if not by birth, then by instinct and aptitude. Mistakes. The place stank of weakness, waste, and defeat. He detested it. And he was annoyed he had been made to come here. He was better than this. Kolm had never been defeated. But, he reminded himself, some jobs just could not be delegated. So, it was up to him.

Inside, the stink became even worse – no longer just an allegorical aroma, but an all too real and putrid one. The unclean scent of sweat mixed with what – urine? really? It accosted his nostrils: the thin, dry, rancid smell of futility laced with trepidation, fear, and foreboding. He remembered it well. An animal odor. The condemned had reeked of it.

How very far away he was from the lakes and forests of boyhood. How could such richness and beauty exist in the same world as these filthy halls? How could the strong, independent people of the mountains exist in the same world as the broken, irrelevant corpses who inhabited this hopeless place and places like it?

How could such pure terrain as he'd known during childhood exist in the same world as these grossly contorted and decimated city blocks, these dank places where people did not live but instead merely existed, and where rats competed with men for dominance?

How could the richness of those rural communities, the tightly woven and beautiful fabric of people and place, exist in the same world as this reverse image: this aberration? Positive and negative. The difference between a Schubert waltz and the discordant, heroin-laced black Jazz with which mongrel America infected the world.

Two flights up he encountered several old men sharing a bottle. Uniformly filthy. On the next floor he encountered a coarse-looking hooker apparently just leaving her apartment. She eyed him up and down – taking in, he imagined, his fine clothes, his clean-shaven appearance, and the overall suggestion of affluence. He pushed by her roughly and quickly. The thought of such uncleanliness repulsed him.

"Faggot!" she shouted after him.

He remembered the bordellos at the camps. He'd at one point been instrumental in planning, designing, and implementing them. These were clean establishments – in fact nearly as antiseptic as hospitals. He remembered the women: stanch, proud girls specially-recruited to provide comfort for deserving men on whom the Reich depended. These were not sluts. These were honorable and fine Aryan females meeting vital needs, sharing themselves for the good of the Fatherland. The furthest thing from whores. Anything but. In addition to physical release, they offered comradeship, understanding, and relaxation to brave men charged with an unsavory but entirely necessary task.

As he arrived at the seventh floor he drew a slip of paper from his pocket and scanned the apartment number written in Ingrid's hand. 712. He moved past 701, 702 and onward to the very end of the hall till at last he found himself at his destination. A television blared from within. Some idiotic game show with people shouting and bells ringing. The kind of thing dim housewives watched while ironing shirts or washing dishes. Mindless babble of the worst kind. The saddest part? Kolm was not surprised. Not at all. Mediocrity such as this had always disgusted him. Always. For as long as he could remember.

Kolm knocked lightly on the door, stood there for a moment without any answer, and then rapped louder. A moment later he heard movement – a curse, a few steps, the television switched off to achieve blessed silence, and a few more steps.

"Who is it?" came a voice.

"A friend," Kolm answered. "A friend who has spoken with your son."

"My son?"

"Yes. I bring good news. Please let me in."

Kolm heard a dead-bolt being thrown, after which the door opened a few inches, still with a chain on it. The man looked out curiously.

"Do you recognize me?" Kolm asked.

The man stared for a moment, then nodded in dumb recognition.

"It is you!"

"Yes," Kolm answered. "You wanted to see me and so here I am, my brother."

*

Harman drove. One of the young men – Sandro, the boy with the elaborate tattooed crucifix on his right arm – sat beside him in the passenger seat. Alexander and Cristof lay on air-mattresses in the back of the van, complaining about the occasional bump in the highway from which the mattresses offered scant protection.

Music played loudly from the eight-track, allowing little conversation. The ghost of Patsy Cline crooned from the grave: at once distant and immediate.

Harman did not know why he loved American country music so much, but he did. It seemed to speak of things heartfelt, spiritual, and genuine. Such haunting, heartbreaking songs as Cline's "Sweet Dreams" represented the true fruit of human experience. They offered so much more than the usual saccharine, tuneful concoctions which comprised most popular music. In the end it was all essentially tragic, just like life. Thus *real*.

Harman guessed his youthful compatriots would prefer something more modern. But it was *his* van. Of course, Harman also loved the traditional Romani music: the slow, plaintive folksongs; the boisterous dance music of violins and guitar. It was, he supposed, in the blood.

Sandro wiped down his Automag III after having dumped the cartridge of .30 caliber amo into his lap. He'd just acquired the thing, and seemed delighted. A bit fancy and super-charged for Harman's taste, but boys would be boys, and they liked their toys. Harman stuck to tradition. A far simpler (and cheaper) contraption. After all, guns were like wristwatches or sunglasses. Whether cheap or expensive, they all rendered the same service.

Alexander and Cristof smoked cigarettes, as did Harman. Hand-rolled. Without filters. Cristof nursed a beer – his fifth or sixth. Harman was not sure.

Cristof was new to this, and understandably nervous. But he'd do fine. Harman knew he would.

He'd watched them grow up – fine travellers all. He'd known and worked with their fathers, living the life, proudly continuing the nomad tradition. He'd seen them laboring hard picking grapes in Italian vineyards, breaking horses in Spain, and engaging in the many other different tasks and trades with which their Gypsy tribe supported themselves in different locales and seasons throughout the year. He took great pride in them and in all the rest of his people – resiliant, adaptable, self-sufficient. And he nursed a perpetual rage over the spurious ways the popular media always caricatured their race: thieves, char-latans, con-artists.

These misconceptions and prejudices were hard to overcome – often impossible to overcome. But like all his outsider brethren, Harman had grown up with this and conducted himself accordingly. One on one, man after man, year after year, Harman consistently and quite consciously demonstrated himself to be scrupulously fair and honest in all his dealings, whether inside or outside his Romani clan. By this he hoped to defeat the stereotype at least in small increments. No one of their tribe could do any more, or less.

Harman made no stops after leaving the neighborhood of Bonn. The trip took several hours. About half-way through, Alexander handed out sandwiches from the cooler at the rear of the van. The women had also sent them off with fresh-baked pretzels, soda-bread, and apples. Enough to sustain them for one day, which was all it would take.

It was through his father that Harman had first come to know Kreigsman and Rubin. His father had suffered with them at Auschwitz. They'd all three been skin and bones when liberation finally arrived. Their shared experience – their shared walk through Hell – bonded them, and they remained a trio of friends thereafter. Like Kreigsman and Rubin, Harman's father lost his family (well, most of his family) in the camp – Harman's mother, and all of Harman's brothers and sisters.

Harman himself only survived because the SS shipped him off to Essen, on the Ruhr, to slave like so many other children in one of the Krupp armaments plants. The factory where he'd worked still stood, still blew smoke. Through the years, Harman had wryly noted the presence of Alfried Krupp on many national and civic committees and boards, and in Olympic yacht races: still a multi-millionare, still the sole owner of a vast manufacturing empire. Harman had celebrated Krupp's slow and painful death from cancer several years earlier. But the fact that he'd lived out his days with respect, and in luxury, explained why Harman did what he did, and did it without any second thoughts whatsoever.

Sandro, Alexander, and Cristof had all been born well after the bad times. But their families experienced grave losses. (Indeed, what German Gypsy family hadn't?) The memory of this burned like a scar from a red hot iron drawn from fire and touched to the skin of their entire race – a pain and a branding never to be forgotten, healed, or erased. All one could do was salve the wound with the blood of the makers of the wound, wherever and whenever the State would not, or could not.

Harman was nothing if not business-like and calm. He had his passion, yes, but he routinely locked this away lest it cloud his judgment and make him sloppy. One had to be methodical and shrewd. One had to be professional, and astutely calculating. Otherwise trouble would follow. No grandstanding. No histrionics. No lectures or sermons. But also no mercy.

It was 10 PM by the time they made it into Bay-reuth's city center. Street-lights beamed. Steam rose from grates in gutters. A church-bell tolled. Stray dogs ran in silent packs through a small park square beneath the statue of some otherwise long-forgotten hero.

Harman parked in an alley not far from their target.

"This is it," he said. "We'll stay here. I know we're not too comfortable, none of us, but try to get as much rest as you can. We'll go about our business as soon as dawn breaks and then get the hell out of here."

Cristof and Alexander remained on their mattresses. Harman and Sandro reclined their seats back as far as they would go. And at some point, Harman managed to sleep.

*

Harman dreamed of Auschwitz, and of Essen.

In his nightmare he was there all over again – and a frightened boy all over again.

At Auschwitz he was paraded naked, with other boys, before the Krupp selector who inspected their muscles and teeth, as if they were horses. When the boy in front of Harman explained he could not see without his thick glasses – the only thing he wore – an SS officer (the same gruesome man who would bring them to Essen and oversee their slavery) slapped him in the face with a swagger stick, shattering the glasses, shards of which fell into the boy's eyes. Guards led the boy off as they would a blind man – in the direction of the gas chambers. In the next instant of the dream Harman and some 600 other boys and girls stood manacled and packed tight in a box-car for the long trip to Essen. They were fed not a thing until their arrival, and then only a thin soup. Once "fed," they were each issued a shirt, pants, a burlap jacket, and a pair of wooden clogs

In his dream he once again walked through the crowded and unhealthy Krupp camp – Fünfteichen – just outside the factory gates. He tasted the diet of stale horsemeat, much of it infected (they found out later) with tuberculosis, the watery soup laced with a few trifles of turnip or cabbage, and the days-old bread leftover from the guards' mess. The sign overhead read "Keine Arbreit, Kein Fressen" – *No Work, No Feeding*. (Ironically, while the word *Essen* meant "to eat," the word *Fressen* stood for the feeding of farm animals: beasts of burden.)

He looked on, terrified, as Krupp foremen and "shock guards" herded new slaves out of arriving rust-red boxcars, kicking them and beating them with leather truncheons – dragging to work those so weak they could barely walk. He saw the result after Krupp barbers laughingly shaved the heads of young girls to form absurd and grotesque designs – making all these "subhumans" truly resemble what the Reich said they were. He inhaled his own horrible odor, and that of his fellow slaves. Looking through a window into the office of a Krupp manager, he saw a sign reading "Vernichtung durch Arbeit" – *Extermination through Work.*

He was only twelve, but children as young as six labored beside him in Krupp's dark satanic mill twelve hours per day, seven days a week. Some slept in tents, some on the ground, and the very lucky in huts without heat – all the year round. Barbed wire surrounded them. Bored but cruel SS guards, supplemented by the Krupp firm's own bored but cruel private police, circled them: their only break in the monotony being grotesque, sadistic abuse of the slaves, both male and female. This had been the special hobby of the gruesome one, the man with the stain on his face, the one who not only acted but *looked* the monster – the same man whom Harman then and now most wanted to kill more than anyone else in the world.

Many of the slaves died in the bombings of the Ruhr Valley and its munitions plants, but welcomed the bombings nonetheless. The slaves sought what shelter they could in simple, primitive ditches dug for the purpose, or in the somewhat safer railroad tunnels a bit further away, depending on who could run the fastest. *Survival of the fittest.*

Indeed, that seemed part of the Krupp plan. Again and again, night and day, he saw the weak – those not lucky enough to die in bombings – fall into comas from malnutrition or tuberculosis or both, then simply cease to be. He saw others who fainted at their jobs or on Fünfteichen's parade ground (*Appellplatz*), taken away never to be seen again, for the Fünfteichen had its own gas chamber. And he witnessed many instantaneous executions, as when one starving man who'd been set to work clearing rubble from a bombed Krupp bakery was seen by a guard to reach for the black heal of a singed and dirty loaf of bread. The guard put a bullet through his heart. Other less spontaneous, more ritualized public executions (by decapitation and hanging) happened every evening right on the Appellplatz itself, under flood lights. The same went for less severe punishments administered with rubber hoses while all the inmates stood at attention and looked on.

Yes, the ancient and distinguished arms firm of Krupp, founded 1587, manufactured death in many more ways than one.

*

Once a year, always on a special date in early November, Rubin made the long journey from his home in Bremen to Auschwitz-Birkenau. More precisely, he journeyed to the banks of the nearby Vistula River – the grave of his wife and children, the place where the Nazis always dumped the powder remains of those killed. It had been on November 10th 1943 that they'd arrived at the camp: himself, Esther, little two-year old David, and seven-year old Arella. It had been on that date he'd seen the last of them – he being directed nonchalantly in one direction, they in another: to death within the hour. Every year the dignified schoolteacher, who had remarried once the horrors were all over and fathered two more children, went to the spot he believed sacred and recited Kaddish for those lost whom he'd first loved.

Now, as he contemplated Jurgen's quick success, he thought of that family long gone. Little David, like all of them exhausted after the long and grueling ride in the cramped and filthy freight car, crying and cowering behind his mother in the face of the enraged SS men who randomly clubbed people in the long line and ordered them to move faster: *schnell, schnell.* Beautiful Arella, holding her father's hand tightly – her eyes wide with fear, her hand trembling despite his firm grasp. And wonderful, dignified Esther – brave and silent, her head held high, her jaw set.

He had no photographs. Only memories. Most hauntingly, the memory of their backs as they were pushed and shoved away from him in the direction of what he soon learned were the gas chambers. He watched them for only a moment before a swagger stick blow to his face abruptly made him turn away and begin walking – to where or what he did not know.

He often told his new family stories of his old family, and they did not mind. The children, especially, had been anxious to hear about the brother and sister they'd never had a chance to know. He did not dwell on how it ended, at least not while his listeners were still young. Children did not need to hear of such things. Instead he spoke of games and toys and joyful moments. And now he shared the same memories with his grandchildren – the grand-children which the murderers had hoped never to see born in their zeal for the eradication of all Jews every-where.

Now Auschwitz-Birkenau and the other sinister camps were museums and memorials where ghosts walked and whispered their solemn stories to all who came. Now they were somber spots where visitors wandered with hushed reverence, absorbing and understanding the horrors in a way no mere book or photograph could possibly help them do. The camps – with their chambers of death, their enormous ovens, their barbed wire, their gallows, and their stark barracks – the camps now stood as silent witnesses against themselves, and their creators.

Rubin would stand long and long at the point of the confluence of the Vistula and Sola Rivers. He knew, of course, that the charred remnants of his loved ones had long ago ended up in the distant Baltic Sea. Nevertheless he strongly felt their presence here – their spirits – as at no other place, here above these waters and on this shore. He remembered his Isaiah: *Let the inhabitants of the rock sing ...*

Instead of a rock left on a gravestone, a rock cast unto the water. In memory.

*

That evening, Lisel sat in a pew at St. Winfried's. She said a Novena for Dieter – for the repose of his soul, that he might find communion with all the Saints in Heaven, and enjoy the light and love of God forever. Many kilometers away, at St. Eberhard's Cathedral in Stuttgart, Wilfried did the same.

In a Munich tenement, Heinz Kolm (aka, Jurgen Enkert, the elder) sat across from his brother as they both polished off the bottle of whiskey. Kolm listened attentively to his brother's tale of his long and sad vagabond life on the run, in hiding, below the equator.

In a Bonn morgue, the medical examiner conducted an autopsy on what had once been Dieter Ohlendorf. He took blood and placed it in a vile. He cut open the cadaver's chest and sliced away a section of lung. He performed several other standard procedures before he and his assistant sewed the body back up and shoved it into a refrigerated vault, a handwritten identity card attached with string to the big right toe.

In a large bed at Kolm's mansion in Bayreuth, an attractive brunette named Jeanette kissed and licked and nibbled her way down the naked body of Kolm's assistant Ingrid, eventually arriving at the spot between her legs and staying there until Ingrid came again and again in waves of ecstatic pleasure. Then Ingrid returned the favor.

In the rectory of Bayreuth's Catholic Church of St. Benedict, the Confessor smoked a cigarette and drank red wine. He'd just finished packing a large suitcase, loading it with some street clothes, an extra cassock and collar, several guns, and a few other special items he'd be needing. He also packed his little sacramental kit containing Holy Water, unconsecrated hosts, and other implements of ministry. After his cigarette and his wine he would lie down and try to get some rest. The time was drawing near.

In an elaborate Berlin loft, the man who had once been SS-Obergruppenführer Albert Pechstein sat painting with oils on a large canvas. A vast horde of finished projects – dozens – sat stacked against a wall. They were all signed "Steiner" – his current name. They variously depicted trains and smokestacks and other mechanized, industrial images – but not a single human being. He realized he was not very talented, but the hobby relaxed him and satisfied a slight but persistent creative urge. None of his works warranted attempts at exhibition or sale, but he enjoyed inflicting them on friends as gifts, friends who then felt obligated to hang them prominently in their homes. The world was so dull. One had to find amusement wherever one could. He wondered how Yom Kippur would work out, not that he much cared. The Confessor had always been far too earnest for Pechstein's taste. In fact, quite insane and messianic so far as he was concerned. But even a mad-dog had to be let off its leash every once in a while.

At their apartment in Bonn, Jurgen and Ruth handed over the list of interviewees to the policeman who came. Though surprised to be asked, Ruth also provided the raw footage from her documentary in progress, but only after exacting a promise this would be returned in short order, so that her work could proceed. She'd decided to dedicate the film to Dieter, and to make his murder part of the narrative. After the policeman left, Jurgen and Ruth continued their discussion about how to explain all this to Eli, who busily played with toy cars in the next room – content, happy, oblivious.

In Poland, at distant Chelmno, an unceasing, ancient breeze continued its eternal movement off the Ner River. The breeze traveled over the graves of some 180,000 dead, across the site of the long-gone castle, and circled about the roof and spire of the massive white church – still standing tall, still reaching urgently up to God.

Chapter 7

The sun barely peaked over the horizon as Harman and his crew pulled their van up to the front of the grand home. The streets stood empty.

Cristof, the youngest, remained in the van – his job being to stand watch on the off-chance of any potential interruption.

Harman, Sandro, and Alexander entered through the front door. They all wore gloves. Sandro used a battery-powered drill with a strong tungsten steel bit (this manufactured by Krupp) to ravage the several locks. He made quick work of this.

Holding guns in their hands, the three ran quickly through the first floor, surveying each room and finding no-one about. This was to be expected. "Kolm" would most likely at this hour still be asleep upstairs, as would anyone else present – probably the secretary Ingrid.

They proceeded quickly but quietly up the stairs to the second floor, then moved just as silently from bedroom to bedroom. In the last, the grandest of them, they found the two women naked and deeply asleep in each other's arms.

It was Harman who, sitting down on the edge of the bed, tapped his gun on the blonde's forehead, startling her awake. She stared at him wide-eyed, shaking in fear, as the brunette beside her slowly awoke and just as slowly realized the frightening presence of Harman and his cohorts.

"Please don't hurt us," said the blonde in a frightened whisper.

Harman did not take the gun from her forehead.

"Where," he said quietly, "is Enkert?"

"Who?" the blonde asked, seeming to be genuinely confused.

Harman rolled his eyes.

"OK, Kolm. Where is Kolm?"

"He's, he's not here."

"Where is he?"

"I don't know. He never tells me. He's away. I don't expect him back for a day or two."

"You shouldn't lie to me. If you do, I will kill you."

"I'm not. I swear. I honestly don't know."

Harman guessed he believed her. Something about her manner told him she was not the type who would risk death out of loyalty. He could tell about these things. He had a talent for reading people. He knew the sound of focused and total self-preservation when he heard it. This woman was no soldier.

He ignored the horrified brunette who sat up and curled herself into a fetal position – perhaps out of fear, perhaps out of modesty, probably a combination of both – her eyes jumping nervously from man to man to man.

Sandro and Alexander smiled widely – highly amused, enjoying the view.

"Is there anyone else here?" Harman asked, just as quietly and calmly as before.

"No."

"And where are Kolm's records and files? His paperwork."

"Upstairs," the blonde immediately volunteered. "In the attic. The office."

Harman tossed his head to indicate Sandro and Alexander should go. He himself remained with the women. They sat together in silence.

He soon heard the two young men grunting and cursing while they bounced what sounded like heavy metal file cabinets down the stairs. Their several trips took them almost an hour.

"Be sure to get everything!" Harman shouted.

"Yes, damn it! We know, we know. What do you think we are doing? There is also a wall safe. We will use the drill."

When finally the two men returned to the bedroom they were winded, sweaty, and annoyed.

"Ten, *ten*," said Cristof. "And three floors up. What bullshit."

"Stop complaining," said Harman. "We're almost done here."

Alexander nodded to the two women.

"What do we do with them?"

"Nothing much," Harman answered.

He'd noted a closet on the opposite side of the room, and a large, heavy bureau standing beside it. Harman went over to the closet door and opened it. A rack of jackets and slacks. Apparently nothing more. But he double-checked the shelf up top, and the pockets of the clothing, just to make sure.

Then he turned to the women.

"Get up and get over here," he ordered.

The women stood – shivering, naked, their arms folded across their chests. They walked slowly to the closet.

"In!" Harman commanded, motioning with his gun.

"I have to go to the bathroom," said the blonde.

"Good luck with that. *In!*"

The women did as instructed. Harman slammed the door behind them.

He nodded to Sandro and Alexander.

"Move the bureau in front of the door."

The two pushed and pulled the massive thing until it was in position.

"Do you have anything else enormously heavy you'd like us to move?" Sandro asked. "It would have been easier just to shoot them."

Harman knew young Sandro was speaking sarcastically and rhetorically, and did not mean what he said. Nevertheless, he answered.

"We don't kill civilians. Now let's get the fuck out of here."

Before they left, they raided the kitchen.

They found what they were looking for in the cupboard – several cases of good beer, along with a number of bottles of top-shelf liquor. The boys could have themselves a party while Harman drove them home. They'd earned it, after all.

The booze came in handy. As uncomfortable as Cristof and Alexander had been during the ride to Bayreuth, they were all the more so on the ride back to the camp outside of Bonn. The files took up nearly all of the rear of the van, leaving only the tightest space for the two to sit. They used the folded air-mattresses as highly-inadequate seats and backrests. Harman hoped getting drunk would decrease rather than increase their whining. It could go either way. Luckily, as it turned out, the liquor in this instance lulled rather than excited. The same went for Sandro, who in the passenger seat nursed an expensive bottle of rum.

Harman did not himself imbibe. The last thing they needed was an accident, or to be pulled over. They'd nearly finished their mission, but not completely. He would enjoy himself once they were back at home relaxing with their families and friends. Then he would sit back and drink and congratulate himself. Not before.

*

Jurgen Enkert the elder – who called himself *Kolm* – awoke to the sound of a radio blaring in the apartment next door, the noise of it crashing through thin walls. Other sounds came from other places. A baby cried, doors slammed, and a couple argued, swearing viciously at one another. On the street far below, jammed-up morning traffic navigated all too loudly. Trucks rumbled, horns honked, cars started and stopped, brakes squeaked, gears grinded. Everything around him – even the noise – palpably stank of ugliness and mediocrity.

He lay on the broken couch in his brother's apartment. The night had been a long one, full of conversation. It did not surprise him how little Peter had changed. Of course, physically Peter seemed a wreck – just a pale shadow of his former self. But otherwise he detected no difference.

Peter's slowness and lack of wit had always been constitutional. Kolm remembered this all too well: the absence of imagination and ambition, the willingness to settle, to allow events to shape him rather than the other way around. Kolm had sniffed all this out when they were still just boys, and it never changed.

As they'd sat across from each other the previous evening, Peter had been eager to hear of Kolm's escape and clandestine life through the years. Kolm made this up as he went along, and surprised himself by doing such a good job off the cuff. (The story he spun incorporated bits of what Peter had heard already: all of it rubbish. In truth, Kolm had never left the Fatherland. He'd simply worked as a laborer on the farm of a friend north of Hamburg for a year or so, let the storm pass, and then – with the help of comrades – become his new self.) Peter was also desperate for news of family and all that had transpired with them since he'd been away – queries Kolm was not well-positioned to address. At various times since the war he'd heard accidentally through channels of births and deaths, although he had never bothered to seek out such information. He told Peter in which years their parents had passed, but had no details to share. He'd not seen either of them after the war.

"You must understand," he said, "it was and is best for the family that they honestly believe me dead. *Total* separation. For this reason they've heard and learned nothing about me all these years, and I've only heard what I've come to know of them quite randomly – reading obituaries and hearing from a few associates who sometimes travel in our home place and learn things. That is all."

"What a shame," commiserated Peter.

"Yes, yes," Kolm agreed, even though he really did not care. He nurtured no unnecessary familial or tribal emotion.

The Enkerts were all good, simple, hard-working people – and quite boring. They were farmers and laborers and ditch-diggers who came from long generations of farmers and laborers and ditch-diggers. Kolm honestly wondered whether he might have been left on their doorstep as an infant, the bastard son of two physicists. He'd never been able to understand, even as a child, how he'd come to be born into the sweet, innocent, and rudimentary family Enkert, with all their provincial assumptions, narrowness, complacency. Peter was a "chip off the old block." Inquisitive about nothing. Devoid of ambition. Kolm was something else altogether. He was glad to have an excuse to be dead to them, just as they were to him. But of course he did not say this to Peter.

"So you have not been back to Altensteig?"

"No," Kolm answered, in his mind adding: *Of course not, you idiot. Haven't you been listening?*

"I would like to visit. Would it be alright if I visited?"

"I think that would be very dangerous for you. And for me."

"Jurgen ..."

"Please, *Heinz* is the name. Develop the habit. For safety's sake. Try to remember."

"That will be hard, but I'll do my best."

Kolm smiled, but icily.

"So, you were saying?"

"I am not sure what I should do now, or where I should go."

"Well, we can think of something. Or perhaps your boy would have you in London."

"I don't think I'd like London. I've never been to London."

Kolm shook his head in agreement.

"Understood."

He doubted any of the Enkerts through all the centuries had ever gone anywhere they'd never before been, except under duress or military discipline.

"Well, let us talk of this in the morning," he'd told Peter as midnight approached. "I'm exhausted and I'm sure you are too."

Now, from the couch with the new sun shining in the window, he looked across the room and saw Peter sprawled on the floor, wrapped in a blanket, snoring.

Kolm sat up.

"Come! Arise! Get ready to leave. Pack your things."

"What?"

"I'm getting you out of here. This hole is not suitable for a brother of mine. I've a nice lodge in the country where you will be comfortable. A safer and better place. The kind of place you have earned for yourself. I promise. Say goodbye to this dump. You will never see it again."

The trip took them four hours – through Augsburg, Ulm, and then Stuttgart before the road turned south toward the Black Forest. Kolm made only one stop, leaving Peter in the car while he made a call from a phone box. Then they continued.

Seeking the most tolerable form of conversational amusement, Kolm turned the discussion toward reminiscence: their summer days as boys swimming in the lake near their home, their grandfather Enkert who had once shaken the hand of Bismarck (the highlight of the man's otherwise uneventful life, Kolm was certain), the Lutheran Church where they'd both sung in the choir, their mother's sauerbraten, and other similar matters.

Kolm noticed Peter's memories of such things were far more vivid and detail-filled than his own. The younger brother recalled trivial nuances which, though Kolm recognized them when mentioned, had otherwise been long lost to him. The past had worn better with Peter. It had not become abstract or blurred. But then Peter had always been "in the moment," whereas Kolm never was. Although physically present, he'd always had far more important things to think about than their grandfather's banal recollection of the one great man he'd ever met, the torture of being in that damnable choir, or the secret ingredient behind their mother's "special" sauerbraten.

Still, it was mildly interesting to be reminded of these and other long forgotten apparitions from the past. Thus he let Peter ramble on about the annual village festival where the beer was always free; the man from the house near the bridge who talked to himself and bred St. Bernards; the time the Christmas tree caught fire and had to be dragged, in flames, out the front door; and the day the river flooded with the spring thaw, swamping the first floor of the village library.

"What I remember most," said Peter, "is you always being good to me and helping me along, just like you are now."

"You exaggerate."

"No, no. Teaching me to swim. Helping me with my lessons so that at least I would pass. Showing me how to ski. Sticking up for me when the other boys wanted to make fun. And even later, helping me get into the elite corps, and getting me the assignment at Chelmno. You always had me under your wing. I could always count on you to do what's best for me. I know I still can."

"Of course you can. We are brothers, after all!"

As they got near his lodge, Kolm left the highway and continued for six or seven miles along a two-lane road. Then, turning onto a private dirt road, he announced: "Here we are!"

Kolm's private road ran for three miles. After a mile and a half of fairly steady ascent interrupted by a few winding curves, Peter exclaimed: "This is *all* yours?"

"Yes. I like privacy. It is very important to me."

Eventually they came to a locked wooden gate. Kolm stopped the car, got out, and used a key to open the lock. Returning to the car, he drove through and then stopped once more.

"Do me a favor," he said. "Shut the gate and make sure the lock closes."

Peter tended to the chore, after which they journeyed on for another half mile.

Kolm drove slowly. He turned to watch his brother's face as they swung around the last curve into the clearing where the lodge loomed tall. As expected, Peter's face registered in a way which might make one think he was seeing something truly astonishing for the very first time: the hanging gardens of Babylon, the Tower of Babel, or perhaps the face of the Gorgon. Eyes wide, Peter contemplated the lodge with awe. *Amazing*, thought Kolm. *The effect of a mere big house. An object.*

"How splendid," said Peter. "How grand!"

Kolm stopped the car by the front door.

"Come, let me show you."

Upon entering, they found themselves in a large, oak-paneled foyer. Peter gaped at the several beast heads carved into the walls: two bears, a few wild boars. Their raging faces grimaced. Their mouths – teeth bared – rang with silent snarls, as if the animals sought to guard against intruders. Kolm had commissioned the carvings several years before, on a whim. He rather liked them, and thought them a talisman of protection – but of course only symbolic.

"Come," he said, leading the way through the foyer to a vast, palatial living room.

Extensive leather couches and chairs rested beneath a cathedral ceiling. Ladders stood before high walls of book-cases on either side, left and right, on which rested more than a thousand volumes. Above the book-cases hung large and beautiful paintings by masters whose names Kolm knew his brother would not recognize. At the far end of the room an enormous picture window looked out upon a large patio and, beyond that, a view as grand as any on the planet: an astonishingly beautiful display of Alpine scenery – a long valley rising into high Black Forest peaks many miles away.

"My God but this is spectacular!" said Peter.

"Yes, quite scenic. Excuse me for a moment."

Kolm went to a sideboard where sat a phone. He dialed a number and after a few seconds said: "Yes. This is Kolm. Any messages? No? Very good. I will be at the second number for the next day or so. You can reach me here. Yes. Thank you."

"What was that?" Peter asked.

"Just an answering service."

Kolm stepped up to the window and began to name the various peaks, pointing as he did so.

"I've climbed them all. My special hobby, I guess you'd say. Quite thrilling and also good exercise. At the tops you experience such a rare exuberance: a great sense of achievement, high above tree-line, with even more splendid views than this at your feet, in all directions."

"I'd just be happy with a photograph, thank you very much."

"I bet you would Peter. I bet you would."

"How old is this place?"

"Built 1890. The former hunting lodge of a cousin of the Kaiser, if you can believe it. A minor royal. I'm told back in the day many of the crowned heads of Europe visited here for hunting parties. It's ironic, really. The house is designed and built for entertaining – more than 20 bedrooms, 12 baths, a generous dining room and kitchen – but I hardly ever have any guests at all."

"Well, then you should entertain more!"

"No I shouldn't. *I'm in hiding.*"

"Oh, of course. Sorry. I wasn't thinking."

"No."

"How do you keep up with the place?"

"There's a girl who comes in once a week whether I'm here or not, just to disrupt the dust. Also a full-time caretaker lives in a little house further up the driveway. He takes care of the lawn and gardens, and the maintenance of the house's exterior." Kolm did not mention that the man, a former officer of the Gestapo, also provided security.

"Let's go outside and I'll show you a bit more."

A door beside the picture window led to the patio. Ornate wrought-iron tables and chairs, all painted white, awaited a party that would never happen.

Kolm did not linger here. He stepped off the patio and Peter followed him towards what looked like a large flower garden a few hundred yards from the house, on the slanting hillside.

"I love these early Autumn days," said Kolm. "They make one glad to be alive, don't you agree?"

"I've never really thought about it."

Kolm laughed and shook his head. Then he continued:

"My man Berthold, the caretaker, has a genuine green thumb. He loves to dig holes and plant things. His garden is full of surprises, and I rather enjoy turning him loose. He's been with me a long time. I count on him for many things. My man *Friday*, you might say. At least in these parts."

"Friday?"

"Never mind."

The sound of cicadas rose, subsided, and then repeated again and again as the brothers moved across the wide lawn. A subtle wind blew the leaves in the trees, these just beginning turn color and not yet precarious enough to be dislodged. In short, they still clung tenaciously to life, although the old oaks had already shed their abundance of acorns.

As they came closer to the garden they spied a man at work, bent over, digging with a shovel.

"Agh!" said Kolm. "Speak of the devil. Looks like you'll get to meet Berthold."

They walked up a long row of roses and soon came to where Berthold labored. He was a short but burly man with spectacles and a full head of gray hair. Berthold stopped digging when he saw them approach. He mopped sweat from his brow with a handkerchief.

"You are right on time, Mr. Anders," he said.

"Anders?" Peter asked.

"Not important," said Kolm. "I'll explain later."

"And this is your brother?" said Berthold.

"Yes," Kolm answered. "Just like I told you on the phone. Do you see any resemblance?"

Berthold squinted through his spectacles, looking back and forth from one man to the other.

"I suppose. I guess I don't really know about such things."

Kolm turned to Peter.

"Berthold is originally from Bremerhaven. He is a child of the sea! But now he's a rugged mountain man. Am I right, Berthold?"

"I don't know about rugged. But I certainly appear to be in the mountains."

Kolm looked down into the large hole Berthold had been laboring on, then scanned the equally large pile of freshly turned dirt beside it.

"Are you just about done here?"

"Yes. I think this will be good enough."

"How deep would you say that is, Peter?"

Peter stepped to the edge of the hole and peered down. As he did so, Berthold drew a gun and shot him through the ear. The sound of the gun echoed loudly across the valley below. Peter's body fell forward into the hole, tumbling with a somersault which put him on his back at the bottom.

Kolm did not look down. He simply turned and began walking away.

"Don't forget the lyme, Berthold."

"I've got it right here, Mr. Anders."

Back at the house, Kolm poured himself a sherry and brought it out onto the patio. He could hear Berthold shoveling the dirt back into the hole. Kolm gazed out across the panorama of the mountains, sipped his drink, and congratulated himself on yet another in a long line of loose-ends neatly tied up tight.

*

At a rest stop on the autobahn, while the boys – more than half loaded – relieved themselves and washed up, Harman browsed through Kolm's well-organized papers for the one file he was most particularly interested in.

Kolm's precise filing – or more likely the filing of the naked blonde – seemed a marvel of precision: cross-referenced by names old and new, dates, and even locales. Each dossier included extensive data: records of service, copies of forged documents, updated current contact information – in some cases even photographs.

The grotesque face of the man Harman had long been hunting stared out from an 8 x 10 glossy. The man wore his Death's Head military cap jauntily tilted to one side, his smile full of arrogant, cruel confidence. Harman remembered the sadist well – he who had accompanied them all from Auschwitz to Essen, and then joyfully overseen their slavery. Harman dug deep into the dossier to find the deformed demon's present whereabouts and alias. The answer – the manner in which the man had been transformed – left him stunned. In fact, astonished. Harman had thought there were no more surprises left in the world, that he could no longer be amazed by anything he encountered, that he had witnessed and digested every irony imaginable. But he was wrong. Oh well, so be it. It seemed he'd soon be making a return visit to Bayreuth. To the rectory of the Catholic Church of St. Benedict. And there he would settle an old debt.

It took Harman half an hour or so to herd his crew back into the van. Cristof and Alexander had fallen asleep on the lawn not far from the lavatories. Handsome Sandro, meanwhile, had fallen into a flirty conversation with a young – quite possibly *too young* – girl whom he was loath to leave. After many attempts at waking Cristof and Alexander, and much convincing of Sandro, Harman finally managed to get back on the road.

Never mind. He understood. He remembered being young – young and drunk and virile, when being a man was still something new and seemed a liberation. One had only recently moved through a great door into a vast realm of infinite possibilities: a wide open future which seemed as if it would never close in on you, never make you crave an option for retreat. They should enjoy themselves while they could, before wisdom took hold and ruined everything.

Harman idly wondered whether the two women were still in the closet. If not, then what they were saying, and to whom. Not that it mattered.

It pissed him off, however, not to have found Kolm at home. Such bad luck.

Their mission had been twofold. Get the dossiers. And leave Kolm – *Jurgen Enkert* – dead on the floor. At least they'd accomplished half their task. And it was not their fault fate had placed Kolm out of their grasp.

Harman knew they'd be quite busy over the months ahead. He realized the file cabinets in the back of his van contained little else but a very long and well-organized kill list. Good thing they were cross-referenced by geography. That would save a lot of travel and gas. No repeated trips. Efficiency. Good German efficiency, as well organized as an assembly line in an armaments plant.

They would make happen what needed to happen, and bring what balance they could to the world. Many ghosts looked on, after all. Millions, in fact – millions who, though silent, demanded payment be made and justice meted out. *Their will be done.*

The boys continued to drink. Eventually they started to (quite loudly) sing an old Romani folksong of the kind they'd been raised with.

> *Let us dance, dance forever,*
> *Turning circles through the night.*
> *Let us dance, dance forever,*
> *Until we come round right.*
>
> *Let us look and remember,*
> *Till the rivers all run dry.*
> *Let us look and remember,*
> *Until we come to die.*

*

Jules Kreigsman had never thought of becoming a Nazi hunter, let alone a killer. He'd never craved revenge, and still did not. But on a warm August night in 1969 he'd come to a realization: He *did* crave *justice* – a thing quite different and apart from revenge.

He'd never revisited the home village where he and his family had at first been ostracized and then later betrayed by former friends. He'd never gone back to look those old neighbors in the eye and shame them for what they'd done. He'd never revisited his place of birth. He'd never surveyed the charred rubble of what had, for generations, been both a happy family home and a thriving business. Never.

Instead, he'd focused his mind on a new pharmacy business in Vienna which grew to become quite lucrative, and on the single-handing of his small 26-foot sloop throughout the waters of the beautiful Danube. He eventually became intimate with every cove and inlet in the most navigable reaches of the flow, from Kelheim in Germany downstream all the way to the delta.

He'd been in the midst of an extended cruise, from Vienna and on through Hungary and the Balkans, when his perspective changed.

The river, as always, was beautiful. It seemed somehow to mock the borders made by mere men as it flowed implacably towards the sea. Likewise it seemed to mock history itself – the river being timeless and having seen countless wars, conquests, nations, periods, and epochs begin and end. All quite futilely. Only the waters and the mountains endured. Slovakia, Hungary, Croatia, Serbia, Bulgaria. The river did not know or care about such distinctions. The river moved with a deep and subtle wisdom – profound, distinct, apart.

Just above Budapest he suffered a small collision (his own fault) with a large Swiss cruise-ship, and was forced into a two-week stay at a Budapest marina while repairs were made. He slept and cooked in his tiny cabin, even after the shipwrights at the marina hauled his boat out of the water and propped her on stands.

It was a drought year. By the time he was able to depart, the river had dropped so low he couldn't get out of the harbor. Another week went by before the waters rose slightly, at least to a point where Kreigsman could arrange a tow over the sandbar. But then, as he proceeded, the river became increasingly shallow once more, imposing great limits on navigation.

River freighters and barges advanced only at the lowest speeds through serpentine channels circling never-before-known islands. Crewmen hung off their bows, taking manual soundings with poles. Forgotten wrecks appeared to daylight for the first time in decades: ragged, broken ghosts squinting unhappily at the unfamiliar sun.

Eventually, however, the rains came and the waters improved. The 62-mile section called the *Iron Gates* dazzled him, the river slicing through sometimes treacherous and quite mountainous narrows. Later on he delighted in the tranquil, level Romanian countryside. Then, anticipating a long trek back home to Vienna, he stopped at Vidin, in Bulgaria, for a fast overnight rest before embarking upon his return. (He was relieved to hear of heavy rains in Austria. At least he'd enjoy more water and less mud for the remainder of his days afloat.)

The little hotel where he ate stood close by the water. The most expensive rooms overlooked the river. Kreigsman did not book a room. He was more comfortable in the cabin of his sloop. The downstairs of the hotel consisted of a quiet bar and a small restaurant. The upstairs contained only twelve guestrooms. The place dated from the 18th century. Just the right amount of settled unevenness, and just the right number of cracks and blemishes in the plaster, made it picturesque: all those attractive and romantic flaws of experience, permanence, and history. Icons and religious paintings hung on the landings and – oddly, he thought – behind the bar. A host of severe Bulgarian saints watched him sip his after-dinner cognac. He hoped they did not begrudge him some relaxation.

Only one other person sat at the bar that evening. A thin man about Kreigsman's age. He wore jeans and a red polo shirt. The hair on his head grew half-gray, but his moustache and beard were dark. The hair seemed somehow out of synch with his face, and in turn vaguely absurd. Uneven. Lopsided. As if he might have cut it himself and not done a good job. Either that or his face itself was somehow crooked. A man in a Dali painting.

The man nursed first one scotch and then another, all the while glaring back at the saints, matching their disapproval with his own. He seemed very deep in thought and did not, at first, spare Kreigsman a glance.

As often happens, however, he loosened up a bit after the third and fourth scotch.

He'd previously addressed the bar-keep in Bulgarian but, evidently having heard Kreigsman order in German, addressed Kreigsman in the latter language.

"So," he said, catching Kreigsman's eye. "You are traveling?"

Something about the man's voice sounded familiar.

"Yes," Kreigsman answered. "Cruising on the river. Sailing. Heading back to Vienna tomorrow."

"You are Austrian?"

Kreigsman shook his head.

"No, German. But I live in Vienna now."

"I am German too. But I live in Vidin now."

"Seems a pleasant town."

The man shrugged.

"Yes, is good I guess. A good port. A good place to make a living."

"What do you do?"

"Mechanic," the man answered. "For the tankers and freighters. You know. Diesels."

Kreigsman noticed a tic or twitch in the man's left eye. A seemingly involuntary solo blink which repeated far more often than the joint blinks of the twin eyelids. This, like the voice, seemed strangely famil-

iar. The voice had a certain unique and weird shrill-
ness. Not quite a woman's voice, but a voice with a far
higher pitch than most men's.

"You lived here long?" Kreigsman asked.

"Since the war."

"It was good to get out after the war. Such a
mess."

"Yes."

"I've been in Vienna that long too."

"Vienna," the man grunted. "Beautiful. The way
the world should be."

Kreigsman nodded.

"The Vermählungsbrunnen Fountain ..."

"In the Hoher Market Square," Kreigsman interrupted. "I know it well. A masterpiece. One of many
in that city."

"It is not so beautiful here," said the man. "Sure,
there are nice ancient places. But not beautiful everywhere, like in Vienna. Still, is a good town to make a
life. I am content. It is good enough."

"I'm sure."

The man ordered another scotch and signaled for
Kreigsman to be given another cognac.

"*Danka!*"

The man nodded.

"So," said the man. "You sail with your family? Your wife?"

"No. I sail alone."

"You like it by yourself?"

"Yes. Very peaceful. I like to be solitary some-times. I think we all do."

"You are right," the man answered, rasing his glass. "To solitude!"

They drank.

"Your boat near here?"

"Yes, just down there."

Kreigsman gestured toward the water.

"You have a bottle on board?"

Kreigsman nodded. The man smiled.

"Maybe you show me your boat when they kick us out of here."

"Of course."

They drank several more rounds. They never exchanged names. It appeared they both had some-thing in common besides being German. They both liked alcohol – to excess. Eventually the bar closed, and together they walked down the short, steep hill to the water.

"You are married?" Kreigsman asked.

The man nodded.

"She is a pig. And you?"

"Not any more."

"Good for you! A free man. Good for you!"

Somewhere between the hotel and the water, at a point right after this exchange, Kreigsman pulled from the mist of his cognac-soaked mind a memory of from where he knew this man. Actually he did not pull it so much as it drifted in on its own: emerging out of the fog and landing on the shore, rather like a corpse amid lapping wavelets. He saw him: a snickering corruption beneath a Death's Head cap. The man stood at the head of a line idly, almost randomly, swinging a swagger stick to left and right, to life and to death. He remembered the smile. The black eyes. The tic. The high voice. And the insolence.

"Good for you!," the man repeated. "You are free of your woman. You should be grateful. Mine is a pig."

In retrospect, Kreigsman would wonder what he might have done had he been sober. He could not claim to know. All he knew was what happened given the circumstances: given his own lifted inhibitions, his booze-fueled rage, and his companion's equal if not greater inebriation.

After they clambered onto the boat they stood in the wheelhouse and stared out across the river. A full moon shown and reflected on the water. With one sudden motion, unanticipated even by Kreigsman himself, he jumped the man, pushed him down into the well of the wheelhouse, and begun to strangle him. Kreigsman straddled the man's body and pushed down hard, his two hands wrapped around the man's throat. He stared into the man's bulging eyes. The tic continued even as the man struggled in his last moments.

Once the man lay still, Kreigsman checked his pulse to make sure he was dead. What he'd just done – and the accompanying adrenaline rush – sobered Kreigsman quite quickly. He thought clearly. He was amazed he'd been able to kill a man, but he also realized he felt nothing about it except satisfaction.

It was good they were on the boat. Convenient. It made things easy.

With the body still laying in the well, Kreigsman cast off his lines and raised his mainsail and jib as the sloop floated out into the current. The wind was contrary, but Kreigsman tacked and made good progress heading toward home. All the while the corpse lay at his feet. At about 5 AM, once he'd made it not only out of the local jurisdiction but out of the very country of Bulgaria, he dumped the body overboard. He watched it float on the black water as his sloop moved away at good speed.

Yes, that night had changed everything.

*

> *Man formerly known as SS-Unterscharführer Bruno Troper:* We had to be heartless. Ruthless. Not just with the Jews. All of them: Gypsies, Communists, the homos, and the physically or mentally deformed: the idiots, the insane. Also freaks: dwarfs, pinheads. You know, all the mistakes of nature.

> *Dieter:* Heartless?

> *Troper:* Yes, well, take the Jews. It is the same today. As a race, they are a blight. We're all agreed. But still everyone has his favorite one or two. His childhood friend. The nice man up the street. Right? So we exempt every Jew who is liked by a German, and then who

is left? You see the problem. That's why I say heartless. There is no room for any compassion. None. It is sad, but that is the truth.

Dieter: You have no regrets.

Troper: Look, we had a mission. As regards the Jews, it was to destroy the biological foundation of the Jewish race. We did our best. It is ironic, you know. Zyclon-B was originally formulated for pest and rodent control. Did you know that? How appropriate. We tried it out on Russian POWs first, at Auschwitz. Very rudimentary. We just put them into cells and then, wearing gas masks, we threw cannisters in between the bars. That was in '41. We invented the process right there on the ground at Auschwitz, we mere totenlagers, while the idiot officers up in Berlin endlessly researched and debated what would be the most efficient and cheapest method. They soon saw we were right!

Dieter: Tell me more about the evolution of the process.

Troper: It became very efficient very fast. A well-run machine. The first Jews arrived in late '41. They came from Upper Silesia. They came at first in small groups. Each daily train maybe held a thousand. They left their luggage on the platform. Then we marched them to a simple bunker we'd rigged for gas. We told the Jews to undress. We said it was because they would have to shower and be deloused. Then we put them into the bunker. There were five large rooms, all with airtight doors. Trained medics administered the gas. After about a half hour all would be quiet and we'd open the doors. There was no burning in those early days. We had a special contingent of Jews, the Sonderkommando, who dug the ditches for the bodies, moved the bodies using carts and carried them to ditches, and did other dirty work. They were mostly under the command of the kapos. Eventually, when new orders came down, it was also the Sonderkommando who harvested the gold teeth and hair and so forth. They'd also inspect clothes and bags for hidden jewelry or other valuables. I have to say, a great deal of jewelry wound up in the pockets of SS. Fact is, not a few of us are still enjoying the benefits of those spoils. But why not? We earned it. Still, most of it, of course, went up the line to Berlin – and from there, who knows?

Dieter: Was it fast for those killed? You say half an hour. Did it really take that long?

Troper: Well, it was actually quicker than that. At least most of the time. There were variables. We could see what went on through glass peep-holes. The time it took for the gas to do its job depended somewhat with the climate:

whether it was cold or warm, dry or damp. Also on the quality of the gas, which varied from delivery to delivery. About a third of the people would die immediately. I mean those standing closest to the ventilation shaft. The others might stagger about a little and scream a bit, but soon there was just gasping. On average I'd say twenty minutes for everybody. Also children and old people died pretty quick. It didn't take much.

Dieter: When did the operation expand?

Troper: The following summer. Previous to that the arrivals were just prisoners from small police actions. During the summer of '42 the numbers increased dramatically. We built an additional extermination site and started burning the bodies in the ditches. Later on we installed several crematoria. Himmler wanted a level of annihilation so complete that in retrospect there would be no way to forensically deduce exactly how many people had been killed. Word trickled down. I understand he was very firm about this, even though the record-keeping continued as usual.

Dieter: So every single arrival was killed.

Troper: Well, initially, yes. But then German Jews started arriving, and it was ordered that all able-bodied men and women were to be spared to work in the armaments plants. It was about this time, also, that Auschwitz-Birkenau became strictly a camp for German Jews. At least in theory. Actually, some non-Germans arrived on occasion.

It was funny. At the selections, the SS doctors and the officers from the Labor Department always argued. The SS wanted to kill as many Jews as possible as quickly as possible. The Labor officers wanted to obtain as many workers as possible. There was this tension between them. The debates could become quite absurd – right there with people standing in line. The only areas where they agreed were in pre-serving any Jewish doctors, and also those Jews especially capable of admin-istration, such as accountants.

I'll say this. We were glad when the crematoria were finally built. The burning in the trenches was inefficient, and it raised a stench throughout the whole area. Also, the anti-aircraft per-sonnel nearby complained the open burning could be seen too clearly at night. Each of the two larger crematoria had five ovens, and each could dispose of about 2,000 corpses every twenty-four hours. The crematoria also had under-ground dressing rooms and gas cham-bers immediately beneath them which could hold about 3,000. Bodies were brought up for burning via elevator. Quite an ingenious design. Two smaller crematoria could eliminate approximately 1,500 bodies in every twenty-four hours, mostly those killed in the old original gassing bunker. Eventually our combined facilities allowed us to process 9,000 people every twenty-four hours.

By the way, here's an interesting detail for you. The ashes were ultimately crushed down to powder. We then loaded large kegs filled with the powder onto trucks and took them to the Vistula River, where we dumped them out. The Vistula is the world's largest Jewish cemetery, though few even realize it! You don't see that in the books.

Dieter: Elaborate on what you began to talk about yesterday, regarding the degraded camp conditions and the inefficiencies from on-high which caused them.

Troper: Yes, well, as time and the war went on, Himmler began to insist that more and more Jews be supplied as laborers. So, the SS doctors were forced to select a lot of men and women for labor whom they would have otherwise selected for gassing. In fact, they eventually functioned under a direct order saying any incoming prisoner whom they believed could be put into condition to work within six weeks of arrival should be exempted from immediate gassing and put on special rations to make them healthy. At the same time, we were running out of barrack space. We had next to no medical supplies. And every month the Ministry of Food cut the camp's allowance. So what we wound up with were a bunch of starving, sick inmates in an overcrowded camp full of dysentery and disease. All because there was no coordination at the top. You understand?

Dieter: Tell me about the kapos. From what I've heard, they were true scum.

Troper: Well, of course, that's true. But sometimes being cruel involved also being kind when it suited their purpose. For example, with those destined to die they were generally quite gentle and re-assuring, because it made the job easier for the kapos themselves if all remained calm. The arrivals would trust them, because they were fellow Jews. And so the kapos would reassure them. But smartly. With a subtleness. I mean, they'd be sly and say things in the way of indirect reassurance. Like they'd tell the arrivals to neatly fold their clothes and, most importantly, be sure to re-member where they placed their clothes in the changing room, so they'd be able to find them easily after the showers. Ingenious, right?

Dieter: Yes. Quite.

Troper: But then in the camp they were usually brutes. No emotion. No feeling. It was the kapos who revealed the true nature of that race, that's for sure. And damned lazy, to tell you the truth. The Jews I liked best were the ones who worked well and hard. And there were quite a few of these assigned to the factories both inside and outside the camp.

I truly believe most of them enjoyed the work. It kept them busy and gave them a measure of self-satisfaction and pride. It also allowed them hours when they could forget about their predicament by focusing on something else, a genuine task. There is a joy for anyone in doing something well, is there not? A sense of accomplishment. In a way, work sets one free, does it not? That's the way I always interpreted the sign above our gate. It was very true in that way. *Arbeit Macht Frei.*

Dieter: So, looking back. No qualms.

Troper: Look, what great society has ever been built on anything but bodies, bones, and blood? Name one. What great civilization has not had at its base some brutal conquest: some great crime? Cut the crap. Ask the American Indians about extermination, not that they were fit for anything else. See what they have to say. But that's the irony. Some American prosecutor at Nuremberg throwing stones! And Stalin? Please. He made Hitler look like an amateur.

Dieter: How do you see where we are now?

Troper: We are pathetic. The East is its own tragedy. Here in the West we are nothing but an orgy of greed and self-interest, an explosion of bankers and car-makers. Materialism. There is no honor. I will always say it loudly: I believed in National Socialism, and I still believe. You know, you talk to people today in Germany and you can't hardly find a single person who voted for Hitler. You see, everyone is lying. Sure, most Germans feel guilt over the war. But their guilt, truth be told, is guilt over the fact that we lost. Nothing else.

Chapter 8

Early in the AM, just as Harman and his crew made their way into Kolm's Bayreuth mansion, a nervous Jurgen Todt sat anxiously in a straight-back chair beside the investigating commander's desk – this to the side of about a dozen other such desks which took up a large, unlovely, and antiseptic second-floor room.

Uniformed officers and detectives walked about, some holding cuffed drunks or thieves or hookers by the arm, escorting them to cells or bookings or court. Detectives sat at desks, variously smoking cigarettes, speaking on phones, typing paperwork, or simply staring at the ceiling. (Happily, Jurgen did not see the one he remembered from the day before, the one whom he did not trust.) Here was the standard pace of the standard morning in the standard police squadron one might find anywhere – the same impersonal institutional rhythm. Bored professionals dealing with the boring humdrum of monotonous, uninteresting crime. Cynical men sanguinely shoveling sand against the tide.

"So, Mr. Todt," the commander said, "what can I do for you?

He was a man about thirty years Jurgen's senior – distinguished, and well mannered. He wore a large handlebar mustache and squinted at Jurgen through thick glasses, as if still making a great effort to simply see despite the apparently great ambition of his opthalmic prescription.

"I have information which might relate to my friend Dieter Ohlendorf's murder," Jurgen said. "Information which I did not want to share with the detective yesterday, frankly because of his unsympathetic manner, but which may well be important."

The commander sighed.

"The man you are speaking of has never been to charm school, and I apologize. Your's is not the first complaint we've had. He is, I'm afraid, as gruff as they come. If you were uncomfortable, then it was right of you to come to me, his superior, with any confidence you might want to share."

This was just the type of response Jurgen had been hoping for. So he dove in.

He did not mention *Those Who Will Not Forget*, and frankly he had no knowledge of what they would be doing, or when they would act, as regards the information he'd given them. He spoke only of his true identity, his visit to his father, and his visits with Rath and with his uncle, alias Kolm. "I was intending," he lied, "to inform authorities about both my uncle and my father. I've just been taking it all in. I'm no Nazi."

It did not surprise the commander to learn Todt was no Nazi. It did extremely surprise him, however, to learn Todt was in reality the namesake and nephew of the infamous Jurgen Enkert, and that he had managed a rare face-to-face with none other than Heinz Kolm himself. Even more astonishing, that Todt had deduced Kolm to be none other than his fugitive uncle – something not even the commander had known. (And the commander certainly knew much more than this young man might suspect.)

"I felt I had to tell you. I don't know if it means anything. Neither my uncle nor anyone else in that circle knows who I actually am, or any connection I might have with Dieter or anyone else here in Bonn. They know nothing of Jurgen Todt. At least they shouldn't – not if I did things right."

The commander guessed incorrectly that Todt – or Enkert – was probably wrong here. Nevertheless he wondered: If Kolm had figured things out, why had Ohlendorf become a target rather than Todt? He could not understand what was going on. And he did not like to not understand things. He detested uncertainty. The unknown. It felt precarious; and it usually was.

"You were right to tell me," he said to Jurgen. "Keep me informed if you hear from your uncle or anyone else. Meanwhile, leave everything to me. I will follow up every lead. *I will make sure everyone here does his best to get to the bottom of things.*"

"Just please don't do anything that will cause my uncle to know where I am, if he doesn't already. I don't want to put my family at risk."

"Of course not. Have no worries. Now you will have to excuse me so I can get to work on this."

"Yes. *Donka.*"

Once Todt was gone, the commander immediately made a call to the only number he had for Kolm – the man's answering service. He gave his name and number. "Please get in touch with Mr. Kolm directly, immediately, and tell him he must call me as soon as possible regarding a matter of the utmost urgency. Tell him I will stay by my phone until I hear from him. The sooner the better."

As he sat and waited, the detective ran through all the tangled, confusing facts with which he'd been presented. Most importantly, he tried to sort out whether or not there might be any risk in this for *him*.

Overall, he thought not. The only person in the equation who possessed any knowledge of his history was Kolm, whom he now knew to be Jurgen Enkert. And, well, no-one needed worry about Kolm. And all this crap with Jurgen Todt/Enkert, and the wife with her film, and the dead Ohlendorf, had nothing to do with the commander. He began to relax, but he still did not like the uncertainty. Obscure, partial knowledge was no knowledge at all, and dangerous. Its fragmentary pieces were sharp and could cut deeply, sometimes fatally, if one were not careful. Especially when combined with fragmentary pieces of the past.

And the past was all around him.

As a young Gestapo officer he'd worked in this very building, in fact this very room. Of course, back then his focus had not been the normal run of thugs and thieves. No. The targets then were political criminals and racial misfits. The room where today many quite benign interrogations took place – so often producing dismal and disappointing results – had once been far more productive as a place of torture.

The basement where today a small arsenal of guns and riot-gear found storage had in those early days been a handy place for summary executions.

He felt himself something of a changeling. It had been astonishingly easy for him to evolve from a wanted man to a respected officer of the law. Just a phone call or two, and it was done. That was years ago. And now, near the end of a long career and several transfers and promotions, here he was back in the same old building doing much the same old thing. What was more, looking about the room, he saw several of his colleagues from those old times. Even now, all these years later, he missed the long black leather jacket. That, and the power to do absolutely anything he wanted, whenever he wanted, to just about anyone he wanted.

It was only minutes before the telephone on his desk began to ring.

*

At that very same moment, the Confessor drove out of Bayreuth in the early morning light, heading towards Bonn.

As he drove, he thought about the world he would so soon change. The world of innocent children and pious old women – not to mention other frauds and delusions of all kinds. The world of lies concocted by the Jews.

Innocent children. The Confessor did not believe in the phrase now any more than he had while tending his duties in the camps, where he'd more than once shot or strangled with his bare hands those who broke out of line and fled toward some illusory redemption which existed only in their minds.

Innocent children. Who could deny the great capacity of children for steadfast cruelty? He'd tasted it, understood it. He'd known from early on the talent (and desire) children possessed for condemning outsiders, for torturing the different and the weak. He remembered stones thrown by his peers as he cowered against a wall. He remembered being grabbed, his head pulled roughly back by the hair, as he was forced to display his hideous mask for curious newcomers. He remembered snickers in class when it was his turn to stand and do a recitation. He remembered beatings by bands of boys, and their commands that he stay well away from their fields of play, where freaks were not welcome. He remembered suggestions that he join a travelling carnival – where he'd feel at home in the sideshow amongst bearded ladies, goat-faced boys, and tattooed geeks.

But then it was he – the grotesque, the outcast – who ultimately survived and endured despite the taunts and cat-calls, despite the snickering of adolescent girls, despite the isolation. He'd learned his lesson well. In the end, no dividing line truly existed between beauty and ugliness. The only real border lay between strength and weakness, power and its absence.

*

The senior Enkert – alias Kolm, alias Anders – sat on his patio wearing pajamas, a robe, and slippers. Coffee and a telephone rested on the wrought-iron table before him. Once he'd heard what the commander had to say, he'd slammed the receiver down onto its cradle and immersed in a deep rage colored with both frustration and confusion.

He did not know what repulsed and disgusted him more, the fact of his own flesh and blood, his own nephew, being a traitor to his heritage – not to mention the husband and father of Jews – or his own foolishness in letting down his guard.

Kolm, now Anders, fumed with a fierce anger of the type he normally never allowed himself. The degree and level of deceit overwhelmed him and made him almost want to seek something he usually never bothered with: *revenge*. Almost, but not quite. He'd always considered revenge to be a cheap and dangerous indulgence. Something a logical, pragmatic man must recognize as a stupid, emotion-driven extravagance – one not worth any cost or risk it might incur.

The entity formerly known as Kolm? Dead. As of this moment, completely blown. How long until the Bayreuth house fell to a raid? It might well be under surveillance right now. Just dumb luck that he was not trapped there at this very moment. He dared not even phone Ingrid to warn her, lest the line be tapped. (On the other hand, he did not worry much about traces. His line here at the lodge routed through Copenhagen, Paris, Madrid, and several other places before finally looping back to Germany.)

Once authorities entered the house, his files would stand revealed and all mentioned in them become at risk. Such was the catastrophe his interloping nephew had caused. He felt invaded, and after all this time found it hard to believe. He'd been so impervious and untouchable for so long, any other condition seemed somehow not truly real.

Of course, he'd be reasonably comfortable going forward in the skin of Heinz Anders, even though at the moment he felt a rather profound and distracting sense of dislocation. One annoyance: He'd now have to develop an entirely new back-up identity for himself – a precaution in case Anders ever suffered a similar betrayal as had Kolm. He would have to think about that. Thank God for the cash. Anders possessed a liquidity even greater than Kolm's.

Still, he'd rather enjoyed Heinz Kolm, his fine house, his beautiful assistant, and his congenial life in Bayreuth. He would miss the man. In a sense, he mourned Kolm as much as if he were in a box headed for the cemetery. One would be tempted to say a word or two over the dead, but of course the imaginary, fabricated Kolm had no soul. That was the truth of the matter.

He thought of Peter. *Yes, my brother. Once again you've proven yourself a nuisance. Even in the ground, from your grave in the garden, you cause me trouble.*

He grieved seriously for Kolm, but for Peter not at all.

He made only a single phone call. All the others named in his dossiers would sadly be on their own. He dialed and after three rings heard a pick-up.

"This is Anders," he announced.

"Yes?" responded the man at the other end, already understanding a significant part of what was being told him.

"I am wondering whether you have heard from our friend in Bayreuth. He seems to have disappeared. No one knows where."

"I'm sorry to hear that. I haven't the foggiest. Whatever has happened, I certainly wish him well. And what about his associate, the priest?"

"I'm getting word to the holy man. All of that must be *kaput*. Too risky now."

"Make *sure* he understands. He won't take it well."

"I'll communicate this not only to him, but to his staff directly."

"A very good idea. I agree. Alright. *Donka. Auf wiedersehen.*"

"Yes. *Auf wiedersehen.*"

*

SS-Obergruppenführer Albert Pechstein did not rush. He never rushed. At least not anymore.

He'd most certainly leave the hideous paintings behind. Why not? He could always make more.

He would also leave most everything else. Nearly all objects, just like nearly all people, were dispensable.

He showered, shaved, and put on his grey double-breasted suit – the one he liked best and therefore wanted to keep. Also his favorite blue tie and his brown suede shoes.

The safe in his bedroom yielded several forms of identification in several languages, all using several different names. These included no less than four passports – not one of them German. The fraudulent names represented spectral apparitions who, taken together, formed the board of an international trust of which each was a beneficiary. In other words, he'd be wanting all these fine fellows to travel with him. They were ideal company. They gave much, and asked little in return. His favorite kind of people.

He did not pack a clothes bag. Just a briefcase into which he deposited not only the passports and related paperwork but also a compact toiletry kit, the admittedly trashy paperback mystery he was then in the middle of reading, an address book, and some photographs of his parents and grandparents – for old time's sake.

He was not sure to where he would head. Rome, first, he supposed. Out of tradition if nothing else. And from there? Who knew? He'd had quite enough of South America, thank you very much. Besides, he hated the idea of that cliché. He'd rather die than just be one more old war criminal stuck in some shack surrounded by a sweltering jungle. He'd leave that kind of thing to Mengele, who deserved it.

No, he'd seek something more congenial. The West Indies? Or maybe Madrid, where lurked a good friend he could count on. He'd figure it out as he went along. No need for rash decisions.

He'd miss this place, this nice loft apartment, but it would not be a total loss. He rented it from the trust controlled by the gentlemen in his briefcase. They would eventually arrange to sell it from abroad, once they realized their unreliable tenant had abandoned both the apartment and his deposit.

He looked forward to autumn in the Eternal City – so much better than Rome's stifling summer, yet still mild. This timing worked well. In fact it could not be better.

Pechstein prided himself on being able to see the positive side of nearly any development. The collapse of the Reich, for example. Even though it turned him into a fugitive, it also freed him from having to take orders from idiots: Goebbels, Himmler, and the rest – each one dumber and more insane than the next – with Hitler sitting on high as the supreme cuckoo, the ultimate fantasist.

Right from the start Pechstein had considered the Nazi movement a terminal case. There was no way such a sideshow of dullards could last. But Pechstein loved the absurd. The rise and the fall – each had been splendid in its own way, the very best in macabre entertainment.

He certainly did not mourn it. This was why he spent so little time with, and gave so little credence to, those true believers who returned again and again to cry at the bier and pray for resurrection. *One regime comes, another passeth away.* And all regimes – each and every one, everywhere in the world – were nothing but shit. Shit wrapped in speeches, sanctimoniousness, and flags. You just had to take them or leave them as they came. Pechstein generally chose to leave them.

Rome beckoned.

He imagined he would stay at the Hotel International on the Via Sistina – a hostel which had never before failed to please him. Bishop Alois Hudal, whom he would have felt obligated to visit and perhaps stay with in that city were he still alive, happily wasn't. Pechstein had been thankful for the man's help long ago, but disliked his dogmatism. Even worse, the impoverished Franciscan Monastery where he'd hidden Pechstein and the others stood notably devoid of amenities. Abstinence from worldly pleasures was a practice with which Pechstein had little sympathy. Whatever great truths there were to contemplate (and he did not believe there were many), he would prefer to consider them from the comfort of an upholstered chair while sipping an extra-dry martini.

Pechstein was grateful for the call from Kolm. Or was it Anders? Yes, of course, Heinz Anders. They were each on the others' short list of those deserving respect. Perhaps even just a slim slice of affection. In a world where no-one could be counted upon, they'd always had each others' backs. Anders could easily have left Pechstein exposed, with his cock in his hand, but didn't. And there you had it. Such a shame they would never meet or talk again. At least not in this life.

Pechstein gave the loft one long last appraising glance; then he picked up his attaché and left. Once down on the street, he hailed a cab and directed the driver to take him to the airport.

As they drove, he took in the scenery of Berlin for what he guessed would be the last time. He did so in the most detached manner, without emotion. He remembered reading once how Oscar Wilde, on his death-bed and quite out of his mind, uttered the last words: "One steamboat is quite like another." It was the same with places. Differing landscapes and architecture were pleasant to observe, and differing cuisines enjoyable to sample. But these things were entirely aesthetic and cosmetic. He never paid attention to people who spoke of the "soul" of a place. Places did not have souls. Underneath it all, when one truly dug deep, every place was the same place – with only one way of truly leaving.

*

11 AM:
The police commander looked at the telephone number scrawled on his note-pad: the number given

him by Kolm. He recognized the number as belonging to an exchange just outside the city, in the eastern suburbs. As instructed by Kolm, he dialed the number. When a man answered, the commander repeated the words Kolm had dictated even though he was oblivious as to their meaning. "Your performance has been cancelled and you are at risk. Clear out now. Leave."

Setting down the phone on the other end of the line, a fat man in a neglected warehouse on the sad industrial outskirts of eastern Bonn pondered the words. The fat man had once overseen gassings at Auschwitz-Birkenau. More recently, he'd spent several months assisting Waldheim, getting this ragged little platoon of misfits into shape. Twenty or so men – some of them old, some of them young, all of them dangerous – lounged about on cots or sat at tables playing cards. Several smoked. Others drank coffee. Not a few nursed hangovers from the night before.

The guns and ammunition and grenades were all secured in lockers tucked snugly into a corner of the warehouse. Only the fat man had the key. The pay and identity packets were also secure, locked into the trunk of the fat man's Volvo. Each envelope held papers, tickets, and – most importantly – cash. The fat man went to the Volvo and opened the trunk. Then he pulled out the box containing the packets – each with a man's named scrawled across the exterior.

"Come!" he shouted. "Gather round."

The little army assembled, all curious and all – by nature – wary.

"Something has gone wrong" said the fat man without excitement or drama. "I don't know what, but *something*. We've been canceled, and this location might no longer be safe. So, we are done. These envelopes contain your visas, your tickets, and your pay. As agreed, everybody gets their full amount, even though the action has not gone forward. So, you will take what is yours and leave now. And maybe we live to fight another day."

The fat man called out names and handed out packets until only one remained – his own. (Wald-heim had come and hurriedly taken his the night before, explaining he needed the papers, and the cash, to make his own final arrangements. He'd not been seen since.)

The men quickly packed their things and scat-tered, heading out the door and up the dingy alley, thence into the world. They said hardly anything to each other. They were not old friends, but rather strangers who'd found brief common cause. Fond farewells meant nothing. Furtive but prompt evacuation meant everything. Survival.

The fat man packed his one little bag, placed it into the backseat of the Volvo, then drove out of the place and up the alley. He did not bother to close the big industrial doors behind him. He half-wondered what had gone wrong. Well, whatever, he felt grateful. He'd not been looking forward to it. Sure, he needed the money and the new identity and the escape, but now he had all three and still did not have to engage. Call it the luck of the draw.

*

The Confessor, who'd already been on the road when Kolm tried to reach him, arrived at the warehouse early that afternoon to find it empty, the doors open. The vans still remained, as did the lockers full of arms. But the crew had vanished, even the fat man. He phoned Pechstein and got no answer. When he called Kolm, the assistant Ingrid picked up the line – distraught, agitated, in fact beside herself. Out of control.

"We've been raided. Thank God Kolm was not here. It was terrible. They took everything."

"Police?"

"No. Civilians. Or maybe Mossad. They were brutal. They treated us like fucking animals."

"Us?"

"Never mind."

"What about Kolm?"

"I've no idea. He went away a day or two ago. I've had no contact. I left a message with his service, but nothing. I've not heard a thing."

"He is blown?"

"Of course! What do you think?"

"Where is Pechstein? And where are my men?"

"How do I know? Can't you see? Everything is a mess. Everything has changed. But don't ask me how or why. I've no idea. This is all out of the blue."

The Confessor realized she was crying.

"If you hear anything, you will call me at this number," said the Confessor. He rattled off the digits.

"Yes. *If* I hear anything."

The Confessor hung up.

He surveyed the vast, hollow expanse of the warehouse. They had not been gone long. The smell of cigarettes still lingered. An electric coffee pot warmed quietly. A radio droned in the background: a voice reciting the news of the hour – but nothing about a Bayreuth raid, Nazi fugitives, or any uncovering of a Yom Kippur plot. He did not know if this was good or bad.

The Confessor walked to the two large, truck-sized double doors. He slammed them shut with a violent fury. The noise reverberated, echoed. A clanking, mechanical cry of rage.

He went to his car, removed his bag, and opened it. The cat-tail whip – the *discipline* – with its knotted cords lay at the very top, above sacred oils and unconsecrated hosts and vestments. Kneeling on the concrete floor, he pulled his cassock from his shoulders to expose his scarred back. Then, taking up the whip, he began to punish himself, his eyes closed, his lips moving. He flung the discipline over his shoulder again and again. Soon the blood came; rolled down his back.

Mortification. Beautiful mortification. He sank into it. He smiled, scourging himself. Later on he would put on his hair-shirt and experience the righteous discomfort of the terrible itching. That and the cilice chain with its metal spikes, wrapped around his thigh.

The practice removed him from the temporal plane – from this gaping, puss-filled wound which was the world. The pain bore him forward, away from the scarred, tragic, unsacred blasphemy called *life*. Only through such suffering could one be redeemed. Only through such suffering could the world itself itself be redeemed.

Happiness, joy, charity. All frauds. All mere anesthetics. Resurrection and purification first required mortification and crucifixion. Blood and pain. Deliverance. *Cleansing*. Such was the highest truth. Such was what the profane world needed – and what the Reich had represented.

Never mind that he'd been abandoned. In fact, it seemed right. There was poetry to it. Tradition. Symmetry. *The cock crowed*.

He would proceed. He would offer up the ashes of himself. He would take the Jews with him, at least as many as he could. He would sacrifice his flesh, tear it asunder, cast it off, and in a great flash of light signal the coming of a new hour, a new order, a fresh beginning.

The Confessor did not need an army.

He felt himself both a prophet and a soldier with a Divine mission – a mission over which neither Kolm nor Pechstein had any true dominion. *He* had been chosen.

He could do it. He needed no accomplices. Two grenades tossed and then – standing in the very center of the confused, disrupted congregation – pushing the button and setting off his vest, taking as many as possible with him amid the righteous flames of the explosion.

He'd intended to use the vest all along, hadn't he? Of course, he'd never said as much to Kolm or Pechstein or Waldheim. But there was no point in the Confessor continuing after the completion of his one great and final task. He'd thought all or most would be dead already, and his soldiers in retreat, before he pushed the button. But this might be even better. A few witnesses would likely now survive, and be useful. Let those survivors tell the tale.

*

The trio of Kreigsman, Wilfried, and Rubin gathered in celebratory mood, each having motored from his distant city to the safe house outside Bonn. It was they who greeted Harman and Harman's accomplices, and gladly received the dossiers formerly belonging to Jurgen Enkert, aka Heinz Kolm.

Cristof, Sandro, and Alexander were glad when they realized they'd only be asked to lug the file cabinets into the first floor of the antique house, rather than up narrow stairs. Kreigsman was seen to rub his hands together, as if anticipating a feast, as he watched the boys drag the cabinets in, one after another.

"What a hoard!" he said. "What a harvest!" he cackled.

The boys had hardly finished setting the cabinets in place before Kreigsman started to dig in, exploring first one dossier, then the next.

"Hah!" he commented to no one in particular. "We've got you now. We've fucking got you now."

Once they were done working, the three young Gypsies sat down on the floor of the living room.

"Success, yes," said Harman. "I suppose. But we missed that fucking Enkert. Who knows? Maybe the bastard had a warning?"

"Who can say?" answered Rubin. "And who cares? He was to be *icing on the cake*, as the saying goes. But the main feast is these files. These are what we've really been after."

"Yet he's still out there."

"Sure, but hey – he's been out there all along, hasn't he? And now at least he's been disrupted."

"I would have liked to disrupt him in a more fundamental and permanent manner."

"So would we all," said Wilfried. "But we have a victory here all the same. Don't be so glum. Congratulate yourself a little. Be happy. And count on it, my dear Harman, you have plenty of 'fundamental' disruptions in your future. Don't you worry."

"True," said Harman, glancing at the cabinets.

He took out a pack of cigarettes, put one in his mouth, then offered the pack to Kreigsman, who accepted. Kreigsman produced a lighter, and soon the smoke rose.

"The first ones we will have to take care of," said Harman, referring to the people in the files, "are any in this area right here. Greater Bonn and Bad Godesberg. The city itself, and the outlying suburbs. This area will have to be the place of the first funerals. This is how we will make Jurgen and his family safer sooner. Until we've got that done, we will stay close to them, the family. Especially after what happened to his wife's poor filmmaker friend."

"Yes," agreed Wilfried. "Of course. This is most important."

"Some will disappear," said Rubin. "If the word gets out amongst them. Once they realize they are at risk."

"Some, yes," answered Wilfried. "But most can't or won't. We are talking about people who have been long entrenched in their counterfeit lives. Everything they have and own in the world – their children and grandchildren, their property, their houses, their careers. It is not so easy to pick up and disappear – not without leaving all that behind. No, I don't really believe there will be any mad dash for the splendors of Brazil. Besides, who knows if word or warnings will even go out? We don't know the details of what we've disrupted, or the extent to which we've disrupted it."

"Wilfried is right," said Kreigsman, still fumbling with dossiers. "Most of these slobs simply don't have the finances to disappear. These are nothing but a bunch of bakers, tradesmen, accountants, and civil servants. Jokers who aren't going anywhere. Quite a scarcity of moguls. Not a single private jet among them."

"But plenty of murderers among them," said Wilfried.

"Oh yes!" Kreigsman agreed, slamming a drawer shut. "Quite a collection!"

Wilfried turned to Kreigsman and Rubin.

"You should stay in town tonight," Wilfried said, "and come to shule with us tomorrow for Yom Kippur."

Rubin laughed and looked at Kreigsman.

"The good Catholic boy has invited *us* to shule!"

"No, really. I am going with Ruth and Jurgen and Eli, just as always."

"Sure," said Rubin. "It will be good. We can camp out here, Jules."

"*You* camp out here. I'm getting a hotel. I like to be comfortable at least."

Rubin smiled and nodded.

"But of course. No third floor cots for you! I'd forgotten."

"Damn right."

"I, of couse, will stay with Jurgen and Ruth," said Wilfried.

"What time is the service?" Harman asked.

"Ten AM," Wilfried answered.

Harman nodded.

"OK. I'll be there with somebody. Maybe one of these boys. Maybe somebody else."

Harman delighted in the thought that not long after Yom Kippur he'd have his own target. He'd go back to Bayreuth and take care of the Krupp priest. Maybe in the confessional, should Providence arrange things so. That would be splendid. Both appropriate and clean. A single shot right through the thin paper floating between communicant and priest, the man with the stained face, supposedly Christ's represent-ative on earth – but of course, in this case, actually not. It would be a good day. Harman looked forward to it. In fact he relished the idea.

*

Evening:

Harman drove back to the the Gypsy camp not far outside Bad Godesberg, dropped his boys off by the fire where other youths danced and sang and passed bottles, then went to his trailer and made love to his wife. He felt powerful, vigorous, triumphant. He sank into her with a wonderful force – she open, welcoming, passionate, and just as needful as he. Life was good, and revenge – even *anticipated* revenge – quite sweet.

Kreigsman checked into the Hotel Haus Hinden-berg on the outskirts of Bonn at Königswinter, across the River Main, with a splendid view of the water. The place was three star with a good bar, where he settled in quite comfortably and drank and ate until well after sundown, irregardless of Talmudic law.

Rubin whiled away several hours at the safe house, browsing files and improvising hit lists on a piece of scrap-paper, keeping in mind Harman's smart recommendation that the real work begin right here in the area of Greater Bonn. He ate a pastrami sandwich procured from a take-out restaurant down the street, making sure to fill himself up with something hardy before the sun descended below the horizon and he would have to begin his fast. Later on, once weariness overtook him, he turned off the lights and retreated upstairs to a stiff and narrow cot on the third floor, where he promptly fell asleep. He did not find the rudimentary cot all that uncomfortable. *Auschwitz* was uncomfortable.

Wilfried entered the Todts' apartment to see Jurgen, Ruth, and Eli gathered at their dining room table, eating a good meal of brisket, potatoes, and carrots before they, too, began their fast. Wilfried sat down to join them.

"Mission accomplished?" Jurgen asked.

"Indeed. Success. The files are ours – although your uncle seems to have eluded us."

Jurgen looked serious, and Wilfried understood.

"Friends will be keeping an eye on you for as long as necessary. They will make sure everything is well."

He couched his words. He did not want to say anything in front of Eli that might hint of danger and make the boy upset.

"That's a relief!" Ruth answered.

"I like friends!" chirped Eli.

"Yes, we all like friends, don't we?" said Wilfried.

"Yes!" the boy shouted.

After dinner, Wilfried read several story books to Eli. One in particular told, in a narrative geared for a child of Eli's age, the story of Yom Kippur – explaining its practices and meaning in a way meant to be digestible by the very young. The book described how this holy day was one when we should ask God to forgive anything we might have done during the year which was mean or untruthful and might have made him unhappy with us. This practice was called by a very big word: *atonement*. As part of atonement, Papa Wilfried, Eli's daddy and mommy, and even Tante Lisel would not eat again until tomorrow night – but Eli would not have to do this, nor would any other children. They could and should eat a good breakfast and lunch. After all, children never did anything that really, really made God angry or sad.

Much later, after Ruth had tucked Eli into bed, Wilfried called Margaret to check on her and say *goodnight*. Then, once Jurgen and Ruth had retired, Wilfried stretched out with a pillow and blanket on the comfortable living room couch, and was soon asleep.

*

The man who was now Anders sat on his patio, drank white wine, and watched the sun go down over the mountains. Beethoven played in the background – the triumphant Ninth Symphony, written when the composer was nearly completely deaf but still utterly undefeated. "This is the mark of a really admirable man," he was quoted as saying, "steadfastness in the face of trouble."

Yes, Anders would endure and outlast everyone, damn them. For all his belief in the cause, his first allegiance remained the one to himself alone. This was as it should be, always had been, and always would be.

He spied what at first glance he believed to be a Golden Eagle soaring in the distance. Picking up his binoculars, he studied the bird more closely and confirmed the identification – dark brown, with lighter golden plumage on its nape. Perhaps a sign? Here, dancing before him at the end of this most tempestuous day, was one of the most efficient and elegant birds of prey, one of the best killers to be found on the planet. A beast of great and fiercely protected territoriality – one most at home at the highest perches, often on remote mountainsides. Powerful. Commanding. Focused. Deadly.

Anders was well aware of the symbology. He remembered from his childhood church days the vision of the eagle as representing redemption, salvation, and resurrection. He thought of the German coat of arms which, though changing through time, had always included the eagle for more than 800 years – even the Nazi emblem: a black eagle clutching an oak wreath, a swastika at its center. Still today the eagle remained, emblazoned on the arms of the Federal Republic.

Resurrection. Strength. Dominance. The man who was now Anders studied the bird closely, and believed he had found a brother.

Chapter 9

An enormous wooden crucifix with a larger-than-life Christ stood tall beside the main gate of the cemetery. To his child's eye, and in memory, the object looked like a scarecrow. But what might Christ on his cross frighten off? Demons, Jurgen supposed – keeping them well clear of sanctified ground. The thing seemed useless as regards actual crows, which routinely perched atop Christ's head, undaunted by the Crown of Thorns. The vantage point must have been a good one from which to spot field mice. The crows' droppings ran down Christ's face. Hard rains sometimes cleaned them off, but futilely. The crows always returned, as did their waste.

The regular visits to his mother's grave, and the prayers said there for the repose of her soul, were his first introduction to the Church. Later on, Lisel enrolled him in Cathechism classes.

As an awed, devout child contemplating the Trinity, Jurgen frequently imagined himself borne away on the back of that grand amorphous thing known as the Holy Ghost. While the Father and the Son seemed quite serviceable, it was the Ghost which excited his imagination and seemed most immediately present. The Holy Ghost lived in the locked tabernacle atop the altar at St. Winfried's. Even more compelling was the idea that a drop of the very essence of the Holy Ghost comprised Jurgen's soul and animated his flesh. The pervasive Ghost was actually *in* him, a part of him. ("You don't *have* a soul," a good priest told him. "You *are* a soul. You *have* a body.")

With the Ghost he soared ecstatic, until eventually the bird turned to clay and fell to the ground, a victim of absurd adolescent cockiness and certainty combined, he supposed, with marijuana. On rare occasions thereafter, the Ghost could still spring up and lift him high; but for the most part the bird slept, leaving Jurgen to make his own way – eventually, gratefully, back to the bird and back to the Church. He considered the experience a pilgrimage, the walking of a long road back to a Faith that had to be earned through trial and experience. (He hoped one day to join the thousands who every year walk "The Way of St. James," the *Camino de Santiago*, the long and ancient pilgrimage trail to the shrine and supposed grave of St. James the Great at the Cathedral of Santiago de Compostela in Galcia, Spain.)

One thing which had never left him – Ghost or no

– was the rhythm of fall and redemption. He believed the latter was to be achieved through sacrifice. These were always moments when discipline was demanded, when hard work equaled salvation, and when Hemingwayesqe "grace under pressure" mattered greatly. He promised himself he would never be weak, never give voice to pain, and never – *never* – wave the white flag of surrender. (As Hemingway himself wrote many years before he put the shotgun to his forehead and made his own profound surrender: "Man is not made for defeat.") From his low moments of doubt and despair, Jurgen insisted again and again upon resurrection: a blessed rise which never failed him – a recurring victorious miracle.

He considered what he'd just done as something of a pilgrimage, albeit it one of another kind: a possibly perilous journey into darkness, on a noble quest. The Grail in this instance had been his odious uncle and his odious uncle's files. In accomplishing his task, Jurgen felt an almost baptismal sense of renewal and cleansing. Fate had assigned him a mission. God had prescribed a journey. And by successfully moving through the tunnel of that test he'd been somehow changed – for the better. Yet another stone had been rolled away, yet another door opened, another veil lifted.

The first slight glint of the Yom Kippur sun cast a soft, orangish glow through the bedroom window. Jurgen had slept well, but now he lay awake, thinking of Dieter, of Ruth's parents, of the families of Kreigsman and Rubin, of criminals lurking in shadows, and of still more criminals enjoying the bright light of day.

*

Harman awoke just as early.

His beautiful woman lay naked on her stomach beside him – her long dark hair flowing down her back, a gold bracelet on her ankle.

He arose softly, quietly, and pulled on his pants. Then he went out bare chested into the morning – a warm one, probably one of the last.

A low fire burned in a pit surrounded by stones. Several men sat around the fire. They drank coffee and smoked cigarettes.

Harman sat down with them.

"And where did you go yesterday?" said the oldest of them. The man wore his long gray hair pulled back and tied with a bandana. His wrinkled face showed the ravages from many years work in the sun; hard outdoor living. On his tanned arm, if you looked hard enough, you could see a tattoo from a concentration camp. But he never talked about that. "You and those boys who follow you around like sheep. Where did you go?"

The old man and the others looked to Harman for an answer.

"A job," he said. "Way over in Bayreuth."

The old man nodded.

"Bayreuth," he said. "I had a woman there once. She was a widow. She treated me well. I have good memories of Bayreuth."

"You lived there?"

The old man shrugged.

"For a while. She made things very comfortable for me until we both got tired of it. And I had work at that opera house. They needed men to ring the curtain up and down, and stand behind the very big heavy props and move them back and forth. Terrible music. Real shit. Still, it was money."

"And then you returned."

"Of course I returned. This here is my life, isn't it? Anyway, that was a long time ago. That widow is probably dead and that music is probably still shit."

The men laughed. Harman laughed.

Children played not far from them. Young boys kicked a ball back and forth and little girls played tag. Some older boys tossed knives across a short distance into a target of concentric circles drawn on the ground with a stick. They shouted small bets in Romani. They also dared, taunted, and challenged each other as to who could demonstrate the best aim.

Soon they would be men.

"Give me a cigarette," Harman said to the old man.

The old man produced a pack and doled out Harman's prescription. Harman bent down and lit the cigarette on the low flames coming from the pit. The momentary rising heat on his face was not so bad.

The sun shown red on the horizon out of the east, making the trailers and the cars and the people cast long shadows to the west.

"You know there is work in town," said the old man. "No need to go to Bayreuth, unless for something special."

Harman nodded.

"This was special. But now I'll stay local around here, at least until we all push on. I've got something in Bonn today. In fact, I have to get going soon."

Harman looked at another of the men, this one about his own age.

"You, Baldur," said Harman. "Are you still interested in helping me today? You know, with what we talked about."

A short man with a big gut, Baldur wore black jeans, a red polo shirt, and a black leather cap.

"Of course," he answered. "Why do you think I am up so early waiting for you?"

The other men laughed.

"That's right," said the oldest one with a grin. "We don't usually see Baldur until noon. You must have something else very 'special' to do today, eh Harman?"

Harman did not answer.

Baldur and Harman had worked together before. Harman knew he could trust the man, just as he could trust the boys from yesterday. Reliability sometimes seemed the very most scarce of commodities. The only thing scarcer, perhaps, was discretion. Baldur thankfully possessed both attributes. He was also good with a gun, good with a knife, good with his fists, and fast on his feet.

"We'll leave in ten minutes," he said to Baldur.

"Alright then," said Baldur. He stood and walked off in the direction of his trailer. As he walked he flung the stub of his cigarette on the ground and crushed it underfoot.

Harman returned to his trailer.

Keeping as quiet as possible, he put on a white dress shirt and pulled socks and boots onto his feet. He accidentally knocked over a small jewelry stand on the bureau, but the sound did not awaken his woman. After slipping his shoulder-holster into place, he took his gun from a drawer and put it into the leather holder. Then he grabbed his black leather jacket and exited, taking long strides toward his van, where Baldur waited.

Baldur ate an apple. He handed another to Harman.

"Here," he said. "You are a growing boy."

"You have everything?" Harman asked.

Baldur smiled and nodded. He pulled open the front of his jacket to reveal a gun tucked into his belt. Then he reached into a pocket and drew out a switchblade knife.

"OK," said Harman. "Let's go."

As they pulled out, Harman honked his horn once lightly in a gesture of *goodbye* to the men around the fire. The men looked up. One or two waved half-heartedly.

"So," said Baldur. "What exactly are we going to make happen?"

"Nothing," Harman answered. "And we're going to try to make sure no-one else makes anything happen either."

"What do you mean?"

"Some friends of mine. Somebody might be out to hurt them. Probably not. But just maybe. So this is all just a precaution. I've got two boys watching their apartment building right now. They've been at it all night. We'll relieve them. Then we'll stay with the family today, inconspicuously you understand, and keep our eyes open. That's about it."

"Fine with me," said Baldur. "Nothing strenuous. Sounds good."

"Yes, nothing strenuous. At least hopefully."

*

The Confessor likewise rose with the sun.

He was naked.

He knelt, prayed, and used the discipline for a solid hour. He bled delightedly. Then he consecrated a wafer and fed himself the Host.

Yes, the day of Atonement: finally at hand.

He had several hours to prepare.

Today he would make history.

Synagogues, he knew, were full of strangers on this Holy Day. Men, women, and families who rarely participated in other rituals of their heritage nevertheless observed Yom Kippur. He would be among them. Just another anonymous face. Just another tourist practicing casual religiosity, taking one day out of the year to barter with God for the wiping away of sins, for the erasure of crimes from His eternal book.

The Confessor went to his car. He retrieved a cheap, black, oversized business suit which dangled from a hanger above the side-door of the back compartment. Once he was dressed in all but the suit jacket, he proceeded to the trunk of the car from which he drew the black suicide vest.

He'd made the vest himself. The device consisted of several plates of explosives surrounded by a fragmentation jacket packed with shrapnel acquired at a Bayreuth hardware store: a random amalgamation of ball bearings, screws, and nails. Once he detonated, the effect would resemble an enormous omnidirectional shotgun blast creating a wide circle of death.

He donned the vest very, very slowly and carefully. He'd made his own acetone peroxide explosive – easy to mix using common ingredients, but highly unstable. In fact, the explosive was known as *Mother of Satan* for this very reason. Any severe jostling would make it go off prematurely. After placing the straps of the vest over his shoulders, he wrapped the belt round his waist and and tightened it until the front of the vest hugged his stomach and chest snugly.

He pulled the suit jacket on over the vest. He'd intentionally purchased a suit several sizes too large, so as to make sure the bulky suicide device would fit under the jacket – and the jacket drape loosely enough to obscure the presence of the vest. The long cord of the detonator dangled down the interior of the right sleeve, the button at the bottom just reaching his palm.

The Confessor reached once again into the trunk of the car. This time he retrieved two hand-grenades. He placed one in each pocket of the jacket.

He walked to the table on which he'd placed his cigarettes and matches the night before. Putting a cigarette to his lips, he lit it and inhaled deeply. Just something to calm him – settle his nerves: soothe his spirit before the game commenced.

*

Kreigsman looked out his hotel room window and scanned the wide Main. The river reflected blue beneath a clear sky. He saw a boat sailing fast on a beam reach with full mainsail and jib, and he wished he were on it.

He'd just finished a room service breakfast of pancakes. Never mind the holy day. He'd done his fasting at Auschwitz – more than enough to atone for the sins of several lifetimes. God either knew this or He knew nothing.

The radio news reported a story of how the city of Munich was hard at work preparing for the Olympics which would come to that town one year hence – the first Olympic Games to be held in Germany since 1936. Kreigsman thought this a good omen for the future. The turning of a corner. He looked forward to attending at least a few of the events, and especially to cheering on the Israeli team.

He washed and, as he did, wondered who was the man who stared back at him from the mirror – the man who looked so much like his grandfather. The same white hair. The same blue eyes. The same thin lips.

It seemed his dead were always stalking him some way or another. He welcomed this. He felt them just as certainly as he felt the heat of the sun on his skin and the pulse of autumn breezes across his face. The sun was their warmth, the wind their breath. And when he sailed it was the breath of those blessed ghosts which lifted him and carried him across waters forever Holy.

He would remember them today at the synagogue. They would be with him, just as usual.

Before he donned his dress jacket he pulled on a shoulder holster in which rested his throwing and fighting dagger. Personally, he was not one for guns, but he still liked to have an option. He was very good at throwing. He could easily hit the heart of a target at twenty feet or more. Sure, he'd never used the skill. But one never knew.

*

Rubin woke at 8 AM. His back ached from sleeping on the cot. In retrospect, he thought himself stupid for not following Kreigsman's lead and opting for a comfortable hotel. Next time he'd not be so self-denying. He'd leave these upstairs sleeping quarters for Harman and his crew, for use whenever required. (The Gypsy camp was not always so close as at the moment.)

He was an old man and needed nourishment. This is what he told himself as he prepared a small pot of coffee in the kitchen, burned and then scraped some simple toast, and sat down to violate the fast.

An hour later, once dressed, he went to his car and began the short trip to Bonn. The highway, B9, ran parallel to the river and offered great views of the water. Once in the city, Rubin easily found his way to the synagogue, only two blocks down from the Todts' apartment. Being a bit early, he remained in his car, this parked just across the street from the temple.

He turned on the car radio and listened to the news: the daily American body count from Vietnam, the continuing Israeli security crackdown on the Gaza Strip following the January assassination of two Israeli children by Palestinian militants, and praise for a recent agreement which allowed for some goods to be passed back and forth between West and East Germany: this seen as a first step towards normalizing relations.

Rubin did not take any special notice of the man

in the black sedan who drove past his parked car, travelling in the opposite direction. But then, from the angle where Rubin sat, he could not see the one hideous side of the man's otherwise normal face.

Chapter 10

Harman and Baldur pulled up behind a shabby old Volkswagen stationed across from the Todts' apartment. Harman got out and walked to the Volkwagen's driver side window. He found the driver, another fine young man whom he'd watched grow up, smoking a cigarette and nursing a cup of coffee. Another, in the passenger seat, appeared fast asleep.

"Anything interesting?" Harman asked.

"No. The old man, Wilfried, showed up yesterday evening. And the old lady, the aunt, showed up about half an hour ago. That's it. Nothing suspicious all night."

Harman nodded.

"Good to hear. Alright then. Good job. Go back to the camp and get yourselves some rest. Baldur and I will take the watch."

The young man sighed.

"You'll get no argument from me."

He tossed the stub of his cigarette out onto the street and, taking a final gulp of coffee, threw his now-empty paper cup over his shoulder into the backseat. Next he fetched a pint bottle of whiskey from under his seat, opened it, and took a large swig before switching on the ignition, putting the little car in gear, and taking off.

Thinking again about how wonderful it had been to be young, Harman walked back to the van.

"Yes?" Baldur said as Harman leaned his head in the driver side window.

"As the saying goes: *No news is good news.*"

"Right."

"Come on. They'll be out soon. Let's go wait by the door."

"Right."

*

The Confessor parked a half a block away from the synagogue. He could see the front of the place in his rear view mirror. He'd wait until people started to arrive, and then filter in with them. He'd not begin his action until the place was packed, but wanted to get in sooner rather than later so as to be able to put himself in the very middle of the congregation, rather than at the rear. He wanted to be surrounded by bodies. At the very center.

He noticed an older man emerge from a car parked across the street from the synagogue, then cross and stand near the large entrance door. The man smoked a cigarette and leaned against the wall. The sun fell upon him. He lifted his face up, absorbing the beams with his eyes closed, as if revelling in the distant warmth.

Soon another man pulled up. He parked behind the first man's car, got out, and joined him. The second man had a full white head of hair and close-cropped white beard. They embraced briefly. Then the second man too lit a cigarette. They chatted while casually looking this way and that: relaxed, content, with no idea of what lay ahead. No idea that Death was looking at them right now. Or, that given the idea, Death had as well decided to light a cig. Yes, just one more last cigarette. He breathed it deeply.

Slowly, more and more people began to arrive: stooped elders moving slowly with canes and walkers; skipping children, holding the hands of parents; young couples. All the generations. All the Isaiahs and Bennos and Jacobs. All the Esthers and Reschas and Ruths. Here they came. Here they came to die with empty stomachs, just as they had a generation before.

Some gathered and chatted out front. Some formed a line and entered. The bell of a nearby Catholic
Church chimed the three-quarter hour. Fifteen minutes till the start of the service. He'd just finish his cigarette then head down the block, through the doors,
and find himself a well-positioned seat.

*

Rubin and Kreigsman looked about at all the unfamiliar faces – smiling and nodding to people they
did not know.

"We might as well wait out here for Jurgen and
Wilfried and the rest," said Rubin.

"Of course," Kreigsman agreed.

Kreigsman hoped his hair would not explode into
flames upon entering the synagogue. He had not participated in services for years, and doubted if he ever
would again after this. But at the moment it was necessary to be polite. He most certainly remained a Jew
and a believer, but on his own terms. He felt he'd
earned this right.

"We are making progress, are we not?" he asked
Rubin.

"Yes. Slow and steady. Not bad for a trio of decrepit amateurs."

Kreigsman nodded.

"I've often wondered why God kept us alive," he told Rubin. "Now I know. To do what we do. At least I hope that was it."

Rubin shrugged.

"Perhaps. Maybe. You know the saying: *In Jewish history there are no coincidences, only what God would have be.* So I suppose God would have us here now, and so nice of him to not let it be raining."

"Years ago he had us be in the camp," Kreigsman observed. "He owes us some sunshine at least."

Once again Rubin shrugged.

More and more people came, most of them pedestrians from the neighborhood. The line slowly moved into the sanctuary, but still Rubin and Kreigsman waited for Wilfried and the Todts.

*

Harman and Wilfried smiled and nodded to each other as Wilfried, Lisel, and the Todts emerged from the apartment building. Harman and Jurgen also made eye contact. They'd never met before, but nevertheless understood each other as allies.

Harman casually took a position walking a bit ahead of the family group as they headed for the synagogue. Baldur just as casually took a position not far behind the family.

Jurgen and Ruth walked with smiling Eli between them, holding each by a hand.

Wilfried and Lisel walked side by side immediately behind the Todts.

About 100 feet ahead of them a man emerged from a car and, his back to them, began to walk in the direction of the synagogue. He wore a yarmulke. Had they studied him, his black suit would have seemed weirdly sized – out of proportion to his head and height, and draping about his small frame as if hung from an articulated skeleton. But they did not study him. Not even the ever-aware Harman, who assumed the figure just another member of the congregation going to join his brethren in atonement.

*

The Confessor walked slowly and, had anyone noticed, somewhat gingerly. He did not want to do anything to draw attention to himself. But he also did not want to unduly jostle the highly unstable explosive contained within his suicide jacket. Thus his steps were not only slow, but soft – those of a man on

a high wire making no uncontemplated or unnecessary movements, but moving all the same. His hands
clutched the grenades buried in his jacket pockets.
He'd already pulled the pins. He clasped the grips
tightly. Once inside, when correctly situated and
ready, he'd release the grips and toss the grenades,
which would then explode 10 seconds later – this to
be followed by his triggering of the vest.

The Confessor surveyed the exterior of the synagogue and the people who entered. He knew himself
to be the master of them all. He owned them – each
and every one. They were his hostages; his condemned. They did not realize who or what walked among
them. At least not yet.

He was deep in these thoughts when suddenly
everything changed.

*

Kreigsman was the first to recognize the man with
the stain on his face, still thirty feet away. He could
not believe his eyes, but the apparition was unmistak-
able. That loud, one of a kind birthmark could not be
denied. That hideous brand, rooted in the womb,
called out. The realization hit Kreigsman like a body

blow.

"Rubin!" he said, gesturing with his head.

In a moment they were both, despite their age, rushing toward the ugly and odd stick-figure: the sneering skeleton in the black circus tent.

As soon as he saw them, the man with the stain turned and half-walked, half-ran – headed in the direction of Jurgen and his party, still some 100 feet away. He traveled as fast as he could while still maintaining a somewhat mincing and light step. A precarious balance. An impossible delicateness.

It took Harmon only a moment to realize something was wrong. He saw the figure in the distance coming towards he and the Todts. And he saw Kreigsman and Rubin in pursuit.

Harman bolted toward the man. He'd advanced several yards before he recognized who it was: the stained demon of Auschwitz and the Krupp camp, the priest he'd looked forward to killing.

Harman continued to bound forward and was some fifteen feet away when the demon seemed to spontaneously combust. What had been a man suddenly became a ball of fire with shrapnel of all kinds erupting from him. A volcano. An epicenter of pain, violence, suffering.

The closest of anyone, Harman felt a terrific blow to his left arm, then a moment of searing pain before he collapsed on the sidewalk, unconscious. The next closest – Rubin and Kreigsman, some 25 feet away – received slight wounds from flying nails and other oddments, and were blown onto their backs by the force of the blast. Furthest out, Jurgen and his family stood unscathed, as did the synagogue in the distance and the few astonished, confused congregants who still stood outside.

Chapter 11

Several weeks later, just a few minutes after grim Otto Klemperer left his Berlin apartment building, three muscular men wrestled him into an alley and roughed him up while a fourth, with one arm in a sling, looked on. Two of the men held Otto by his arms. The third man, with an elaborate crucifix tattoo showing above one wrist – delivered a succession of stiff blows to both Otto's face and his stomach. The man who threw the punches wore brass knuckles. After about five minutes, he finally stopped.

"We know where to find you," the man with his arm in a sling – Harman – said without emotion. "And if harm ever comes to Jurgen Todt – whom you've previously met as Jurgen Enkert – or any one in his family, you will be dead. Also that Rath bitch. I and my friends will come in the night and leave you hanging from your neck with your cock cut off. The bitch will hang beside you. Your cock will be in her mouth. So, I'm relying on you to make sure the Todts all remain in excellent health. Do you understand me? Even if someone else hurts them, *you* are the one I will come after. You and that bitch."

Otto nodded. The men released him and threw him to the ground. Then they walked away. By nightfall they were back in their camp outside Bonn.

That same day, in Rome, Albert Pechstein strolled the grand, medieval Basilica of Our Lady. He held a brochure in his hands – a brief history of the ornate church, which he scanned with interest. The place – centered on two rows of columns (for a total of 22) taken from ancient Roman sites – had been built in 320 AD and then expanded in the 12th century by Pope Innocent II. It was he who embellished the apse with six grand mosaic panels depicting scenes from the life of Mary, these created by Pietro Cavallini. Also, not to be ignored: the gilded octagonal ceiling by the Baroque master Domenichino. Pechstein came away impressed – and few things ever impressed him. He would shortly, within a few days, board a plane bound for a destination he alone knew. After that he would never be heard from again.

Far away, amid the great beauty of the Black Forest, Heinz Anders settled into his new life. He would do no more ODESSA business. He embraced true retirement. A complete disconnect. He would have more time now for mountaineering. He thought he might write a book about the natural history of the region – for posthumous publication, of course, under his true name. Wouldn't that be a splendid way to emerge from the darkness, to resurrect himself from the ashes, to show all that he'd ultimately not been conquered? He'd already found a reliable full-time cook and maid. And he'd no longer need a secretary. What about a lover? Well, he would see. He'd heard on the news about what had happened in Bonn, and he did not care.

At Bayreuth, an attractive young blonde, suddenly finding herself without employment, quickly received a new job as personal assistant to Kolm's old protégé Winifred Wagner, the daughter-in-law of Richard Wagner and longtime friend of Adolf Hitler. The blonde aided in correspondence and also helped arrange Winifred's extensive social schedule. This included numerous parties where such notables as Helga Rath, Edda Göring, Ilse Hess, and British fascist Oswald Mosley along with Mosley's wife Diana Mitford, were always welcome. After a glass or two of wine, Winifred usually boasted about how she'd supplied the paper on which Hitler composed his opus *Mein Kampf* – this largely written during his incarceration at Landsberg Prison following the failed "Beer Hall Putsch" of 1923.

At occasional meetings in Bad Godesberg, the group of Kreigsman, Rubin, and Wilfried weeded through the captured files and – per Harman's request – organized hit lists according to geographical convenience. These they forwarded to Harman who later notified Rubin once the list had been taken care of – at which point another meeting would become necessary.

In Bonn, Ruth Todt found herself having to threaten a lawsuit before the police finally returned the raw footage of her film. By that time, much of the footage had been damaged, perhaps by exposure to heat. After many attempts at restoration, she was in the end only able to preserve the sound. Thus the film as originally envisioned could not be finished. Ruth eventually donated the audio to the research library at Yad Vashem in Jerusalem, where to this day it remains a vital resource. She never took up another documentary project.

Over the course of the next several years, a total of 503 former SS and Gestapo personnel either went missing or were found dead throughout West Germany. Most of those killed were left with notes on their persons saying they'd been executed by *Those Who Will Not Forget* – but not all. There were, it must be remembered, two sources of names: the files confiscated by Harman in Bayreuth, and the extensive list of Dieter's and Ruth's interviewees, this having been confiscated from Ruth by the police. Individuals from the first source received visits from Harman and his crew; individuals from the second source received visits from Otto Klemperer.

But it was Harman and his boys who did the most creative work. At Bonn, a senior police commander was found floating face down in the Main. Inspection of his body revealed multiple stab wounds. Several other senior detectives met equally disquieting ends within a few days of one another.

In Bremerhaven on one weekend alone there were no less than four executions. A postmaster who once made a specialty of slaughtering children at Bergen-Belsen wound up in an alley with his eyes gouged out and his throat slit open. A nurse who aided Josef Mengele with his gruesome experiments on twins at Auschwitz-Birkenau fell ten stories from a rooftop after receiving a non-fatal gunshot wound to her shoulder. A librarian who'd once been employed as a ruthless Gestapo officer hunting Jews in the Ruhr Valley got strung up with wire and hung by the neck. A former manager of child slave labor at a Krupp plant in Essen received special treatment. He spent his last hour of life strapped to a chair by men who beat him savagely with batons before cutting his throat.

Jurgen often spotted such occurrences in the news. The crusade by *Those Who Will Not Forget* became famous in some circles, infamous in others. The identities of those involved in the group became popular topics of speculation and debate in the media. Also in beer halls. Throughout West Germany, neatly but inexpensively dressed men and women whispered and gossiped about old colleagues who'd met the most unclean of ends. Organizers of the annual gathering at Ulrichsberg added extra security.

The bloodier and more dramatic the assassinations, the wider the publicity they achieved. This fact was not lost on the trinity of Wilfried, Kreigsman, and Rubin – nor on Harman. They thought the publicity good. "Let those who remain be nervous," said Kreigsman. "Let them be afraid. Let them look over their shoulders. Let them dread the day when they might receive a visit. And let everyone else just remember. That alone is worth the price of admission."

Kreigsman once or twice suggested to Wilfried and Rubin that Jurgen become a member of their committee, but Wilfried always vetoed the idea. "Let him be. Let him leave this all behind. He has done enough. He has atoned for the sins of others." In the end Kreigsman realized he had to agree.

The End

Afterword

Although based on flesh and blood individuals, most of the characters in this novel are (unless otherwise noted) my own inventions. The same goes for many of the more minor places. For example, there is no King Frederick Hotel on the Kurfürstendamm or, for that matter, anywhere else in Berlin. However, all the churches named, and all the landmarks, neighborhoods, and streets are quite real.

I've based the texts of the documentary interviews with Klaus Bauer and other fictional Nazis on actual interviews conducted through the years with such war criminals as Erich Priebke and Herta Bothe. I've combined, refined, restructured, and refocused these to suit my purposes.

Held every October since 1958, the gathering at Ulrichsberg, Austria is no longer a conclave of SS veterans so much as it is an assembly of younger neo-Nazis and skinheads intent on honoring their memory. The appearances of Gudron Burwitz (daughter of Heinrich Himmler) and Edda Göring (daughter of Hermann Göring) have been highlights of past years. The physical place is accurately described in the text. The son of an SS veteran owns the site.

Gudron Burwitz's organization *Stille Help* – Silent Help – is the model for Rath's Silent Aid. Unlike Helga, Gudron has never managed to be particularly sexy. And unlike Helga's father, Gudron's father betrayed Hitler, endeavoring without success to cut a secret deal with the Allies at the end of the war, after which he died a coward's death by suicide rather than face justice at Nuremberg.

In early 2015, the 76-year-old Edda Göring – Godchild of Adolf Hitler – appealed to the Barvarian Parliament's Legal Affairs Committee for compensation for her "father's legacy expropriated in the year 1948" – this "legacy" being some $200 million worth of art plundered from individuals and institutions during the spread of the Nazi regime across Europe. It took the Committee only minutes to deny Edda's request.

In the same year, the estate of Joseph Goebbels sued Random House in Germany for quoting from the Goebbels diaries in a biography. Attorneys for the estate argued that, instead of donating royalties to Holocaust charities, the monies should go to the Goebbels heirs.

The existence of the secretive and sinister network of mutual support called *ODESSA* (*Organisation der Ehemaligen SS-Angehörigen*, meaning *Organization of Former SS Members)*, this spanning from Europe to South America and places beyond, has long been rumored but never proven. But such is the nature of secret organizations. One imagines the ODESSA would, at this point, be largely faded, along with the gen-eration of criminals the protection of which was its *raison d'etre*.

The so-called "Dachau Massacre" occurred in April of 1945. The account given in this narrative de-rives closely from the testimony of Waffen-SS soldier Hans Linberger, a survivor of the "massacre."

It is true that the Catholic priest Bernhard Lichtenberg lies in the crypt below St. Hedwig's, Berlin. Lichtenberg died on a train headed for Dachau after protesting the Nazis' mass exterminations of Jews.

I've based the character of the Catholic priest Schiller on the actual historical figure Rev. Maximil-ian Kolbe, who was killed at Auschwitz after being granted his request to take the place of a condemned Jew. The man whom Kolbe saved returned to his hometown in Poland after the war only to find his family had been murdered by the Nazis. Pope John

Paul II canonized Rev. Kolbe in 1981. The cell where the priest died is now a shrine.

That Bishop Alois Hudal, head of Rome's Austrian-German Catholic congregation *Santa Maria dell'Anima*, created and administered ratlines by which dozens of high-ranking Nazis and war criminals escaped to South America and other regions is a fact all too true and well-documented.

The evolution of the killing-process at Auschwitz is accurately described, as is the geography and killing-process at Chelmno. No atrocity described in the book is without basis in facts accumulated and given as evidence during war crimes trials.

The firm Friedrich Krupp AG – now called *ThysennKrupp AG* – remains a significant industrial conglomerate. After the war, Alfried Krupp was found guilty of crimes against humanity. He received a sentence of 12 years in prison and the forfeiture of all property. Authorities subsequently reduced this sentence to three years, and returned Krupp's property, in order that the firm might be of maximum use to the West amid the Cold War. After Krupp's death in 1967, his controlling interest in the firm became the property of a nonprofit philanthropic foundation named for him. Many viewed this as an act of atonement on Krupp's part. Krupp structured the new foundation to be headed by Berthold Beitz, who had come into the Krupp organization during the early 1950s and soon rose to become Alfried's chief associate and assistant. In his pre-Krupp life, Beitz had gained notoriety for saving the lives of 250 Polish Jews during World War II. (Beitz did this by declaring them essential workers at an oil plant.) For this, in 1973, Beitz received the title Righteous Among Nations, the highest Israeli honor given to non-Jews. Not long after Beitz's death at age 99 in 2013, World Jewish Congress President Ronald Lauder described him as "one of the great Germans of the past century."

Ilse Hess (wife of Rudolf Hess), Oswald Mosley, and Diana Mitford are actual historical figures, as is Winifred Wagner. Following World War II, due to her Nazi past, Winifred found herself banned from her post as Director of the Wagner Bayreuth Festival. Officially, she passed these responsibilities to her sons, but remained quite active in the background. She never recanted her admiration for her friend Hitler.

A while back I had the privilege of helping my two friends Sarah Ogilvie and Scott Miller (of the

United States Holocaust Memorial Museum) put the finishing touches on their outstanding book *Refuge Denied: The* St. Louis *Passengers and the Holocaust* (University of Wisconsin Press, 2006). In the course of this work, I had the honor of meeting and interviewing a number of Holocaust survivors (veterans of the *St. Louis* voyage) living within the very large and long-established German-Jewish community of Manhattan's Washington Heights – the place often referred to as *Frankfurt on the Hudson*. This novel is dedicated to the memory of one of them: Ilse Marcus, born 1914 in Breslau, Germany, who lost her entire family in the camps. Ilse herself barely survived Auschwitz. She weighed only 70 pounds on the day of her liberation by Soviet troops on January 27th, 1945. And so, yes, this book is dedicated to Ilse – the warm, gentle lady who fed me cookies and tea in her small apartment one grey day of spring, and told me her story.

I would be remiss if I did not point out one very important fact: The lion's share of descendants of Nazi war criminals are completely and loudly repulsed by the actions of their forebears. Such scions as Katrin Himmler, Ricardo Eichmann, Bettina Göring, Rainer Höss (grandson of Auschwitz-Birkenau commandant Rudolf Höss), and Monika Hertwig and Jennifer Teege (daughter and grandaughter, respectively, of Amon Göth, the brutal concentration camp commander depicted in *Schindler's List*), are just a few examples as, of course, is the young, fictional Jurgen Enkert.

EJR
Wickford, RI
19 May 2015

About The Author

Edward Renehan has written many critically-praised books including *The Secret Six* (Crown, 1995), *Dark Genius of Wall Street* (Basic Books, 2005), *The Lion's Pride* (Oxford University Press, 1998), and *The Kennedys at War* (Doubleday, 2002). His articles and reviews have appeared in such publications as the *San Francisco Chronicle*, Hearst's *Veranda*, and the *Wall Street Journal*. He lives near Newport, RI.

ALSO OF INTEREST
FROM NEW STREET

Hemingway's Dark Night: Catholic Influences and
Intertextualities in the Work of Ernest Hemingway
By Matthew Nickel
"... will enrich every reader's understanding of Hemingway, the man
and his work." - Valerie Hemingway

Capsized: Jim Nalepka's Epic 119 Day Survival Voyage
Aboard the Rose Noëlle
By Steven Callahan
"Soulful, emotional ... earnest and engrossing." - KIRKUS

Beast: A Slightly Irreverent Tale About Cancer (And Other
Assorted Anecdotes)
By James Capuano
"A surprisingly life-affirming tale." - Susan Sarandon, actress

Hemingway's Paris: Our Paris?
by H.R. Stoneback
"Stoneback's lyrical prose takes the reader inside the soul of
Hemingway's Paris, penetrating the surface of guide-books to
reveal tantalizing secrets." - A.E. Hotchner